BELLMAN CARRIES ON

Bellman spent an uncomfortable night, p. 26.

BELLMAN CARRIES ON

by
K. F. BARKER

WITH MANY ILLUSTRATIONS
FROM DRAWINGS BY THE AUTHOR

A. & C. BLACK LTD.
4, 5 & 6 SOHO SQUARE, LONDON, W.1

MADE IN GREAT BRITAIN BY
MORRISON AND GIBB LTD.
LONDON AND EDINBURGH

First published 1934
Reprinted 1938 and 1950

Australia and New Zealand
THE OXFORD UNIVERSITY PRESS, MELBOURNE

Canada
THE MACMILLAN COMPANY OF CANADA, TORONTO

South Africa
THE OXFORD UNIVERSITY PRESS, CAPE TOWN

India, Pakistan and Burma
MACMILLAN AND COMPANY LIMITED
BOMBAY   CALCUTTA   MADRAS

CONTENTS

FULL PAGE ILLUSTRATIONS

And many Illustrations in the Text

BELLMAN CARRIES ON

CHAPTER I

BELLMAN AND THE "YOUNG ENTRY"

BELLMAN trotted up the field, his stern waving cheerfully, and after him scrambled and lolloped a string of puppies of varying ages; they fell over each other clumsily as they hurried after Bellman, who, when he reached the top of the field, good-naturedly turned and waited for the "young entry" to come up with him.

Bellman, now in his fifth year, loved playing with the pups, and old Deacon, the kennel huntsman with whom he was first favourite, would often let Bellman out on non-hunting mornings for an hour or two, and what a time he and the pups had.

First Bellman would act hare, and lead them a twisting run, dodging and turning, and finally galloping round and round the excited puppies until they were completely bewildered, and so tired that all they could do was to sit down on their little fat haunches, pink tongues lolling, and their tiny foreheads creased in frowning perplexity as they watched Bellman tearing round them in dizzy circles.

When at last he too was exhausted with the game he would flop down in the middle of them, and let the youngsters all swarm over him, bite his ears, sprawl across his back, and use him as a kind of general fighting ground.

But after a few minutes of this, Bellman would spring up, shake off the pups, and make his way to an old disused sand pit close by. This made a capital playground and school for the " younger end " ; the sand pit being overgrown with grass and undergrowth of all sorts, which quite often sheltered a rabbit or two.

Closely following at Bellman's heels was one of his sons, a promising youngster of some five months, with good bone, level back, and gaily carried stern ; this was the only one of Bellman's stock that showed any real likelihood of taking after their father. Because he seemed to be genuinely a " chip of the old block " Deacon had christened him Bell Boy, and he would shortly be sent up to old John Thwaites, whose pack, the Withensdale, hunted over the wild bleak Fell Country.

Bellman as a young hound had hunted there for a season and a half. It was there he had been lost, and after many adventures had succeeded in rejoining

Bellman would act hare, and lead them a twisting run.

his old pack in Yorkshire, and John Thwaites used to say that in Bellman he had lost the most promising hound in the kennels.

But knowing Deacon's fondness for Bellman, and when he heard of the old man's delight at his favourite hound's miraculous return, Thwaites had generously consented to Bellman's staying with his old pack; but that was three years ago, and though some of Bellman's puppies had been sent up to the Withensdale from time to time, John Thwaites had had no luck with them, two having succumbed to distemper, and the other, a very promising dog puppy, had been killed in a kennel fight in his first season.

So now young Bell Boy was to go up to the Fell Country to follow in the footsteps of his father, and carry on the fine hunting tradition left by Bellman. As the older hound trotted across the field, Bell Boy followed him closely, and whenever Bellman stopped to investigate a clump of long grass, or unravel the mystery of a new scent, Bell Boy, his son, stopped too and put his sensitive little nose down in exact imitation of his father, and sniffed away, his white-tipped stern waving excitedly.

After snuffing eagerly, his nose buried in the tussock, he yapped shrilly, Bellman looking on with

good-natured tolerance ; but in a minute or two Bell
Boy wearied of his investigations and rushed after
Bellman, who, with his " puppy following," had
reached the big grass-grown sand pit, and was making
his way towards a certain thick clump of brambles,
gorse, and long grass at the foot of one of the steep
red shelving sides of the old quarry.

Immediately the older hound put his nose down,
all the puppies began to show signs of excitement.

Trotting about on their wobbly little legs, some
of them pretended to do a little investigation on
their own. Bell Boy, however, followed at his
father's heels all the time.

Presently Bellman's stern began to wave, and he

quickened his pace and then his deep bell-like note rang out, and at once all the youngsters stopped sniffing and playing about, and lolloped over to him, just as a three-parts-grown young rabbit popped up out of the undergrowth, and sped away in leaps and bounds over the rough uneven ground.

The hunt was up, away went Bellman hot on the line, and after him tore Bell Boy, his long soft tan ears blowing back, and his voice giving tongue in a high falsetto imitation of his father's. After them came the remainder of the little pack, tumbling over one another in their excitement.

The rabbit, who seemed to be quite enjoying the game, and knew exactly where he was going, led them a twisting hunt, up the steep, sandy side of the quarry, along narrow ledges, and through patches of thick tussocky grass.

It was capital practice for the pups, tightening up and strengthening their soft muscles ; scrambling up and down the sides of the quarry taught them to look after themselves too, as nothing else could have done. Sometimes a puppy would lose its footing on one of the narrow grass-grown ledges, and slip off to roll harmlessly down the soft, sandy slopes, uttering little yelps of startled astonishment. However, they always picked themselves up again at

6

the bottom, quite unhurt, and continued the hunt; in this way even the quite tiny pups learnt in time to look after themselves.

To-day the quarry was a stout-hearted youngster, who seemed bent on giving the little pack a run for its money. After running along the foot of the sand pit, it suddenly dodged through a thick patch of fern and bramble, and slipped away across a wide grass field.

For quite a time after the "cotton-tail" had quitted the undergrowth, the leaves and grasses waved agitatedly as the "small fry" struggled and pushed their way through, yelping frantically as they strove to catch up with Bellman and Bell Boy, who were scudding across the short grass in the wake of that flying white scut bobbing so tantalisingly just ahead of them; but the rabbit, having perhaps just recollected other and more pressing engagements, suddenly decided to put an end to the hunt, and did so by taking a "header" into a large hole in the far corner of the field; disappearing into the mysterious gloom with a last defiant flick of its cheeky white scut.

A minute later Bellman arrived, to be joined presently by a panting, excited Bell Boy. They both peered into the darkness and sniffed the damp,

7

earthy rabbit smell, with wistful noses, while in ones and twos the remainder of the pack trailed in, each pup lolling a pink tongue as it galloped clumsily up, rocking a little after the strenuous " run."

One of the bolder pups even ventured a few steps into the alarming depths of the rabbit hole, but in less than a minute he was backing out into the bright re-assuring sunshine again. It was very disappointing, but as Bellman and the string of pups made their leisurely way back across the field towards the kennels, Bell Boy, who was ambling along on his own, had a " find " in the shape of the mangled remnant of a rabbit, which, judging from the rich full-flavoured scent of its remains, had long since been gathered to its fathers.

This was treasure-trove indeed, even Bellman, generally superior to tit-bits of the kind, sniffed and cast a covetous eye towards Bell Boy's loot, but after a second and more prolonged whiff he turned away —perhaps after all he wasn't *quite* hungry enough. But this was far from being the case with the remainder of the pups, who all swarmed round Bell Boy, clamorous for a share of the tasty fragment.

However, Bellman's son was in no mood for sharing the windfall. Growling and bristling, he

8

lifted the rank carcase and bore it proudly over the grass, followed by a train of eager followers.

This was no vague transitory scent, but the real thing, strong and satisfying; rising richly, it was conveyed back to the avid noses of the "young entry" in warm tantalising waves. Every now and then one of the limp back legs would trail along the

ground, and instantly a swarm of white and tan and pied bodies would surge forward, only to be driven back by the furious muffled snarls of Bell Boy, who, fearful of losing his treasured fragment, lifted his head still higher, quickened his pace, and scrambled through the hedge, in a last effort to shake off his pursuers.

Meanwhile Bellman was making a steady way back to the kennels, a little tired of play now, and ready for a pleasant lie down on the straw-littered bench. In the kennel yard he found old Deacon, and Ben, who had recently been promoted to Hunting Hounds. The old man turned and opened the gate to admit his favourite hound.

" Ready fer comin' in are yer ? " he asked, smiling. " Well, an' I'm not supprised neither, them little varmints are proper 'andfuls."

He unlatched the door of the kennel and Bellman trotted in and made his way to the far corner of the bench where his special friend lay peacefully sleeping in the straw. Stormer opened his eyes and his stern thumped twice as Bellman sprang up on to the bench and flopped down in his accustomed place.

Meanwhile, out in the field, Bell Boy was still carrying his reeking prize hither and thither, closely followed by his faithful band. Deacon and Ben leaned over the kennel railings watching ; and Ben chuckled.

" Bell Boy's 'avin' a drag 'unt on 'is own, seemin'ly," he said.

Deacon's shrewd kindly blue eyes followed Bell Boy's efforts as he rushed fruitlessly about the field, growling muffled protests.

" Ay," he said, " he's shapin' all right " ; and with quiet satisfaction, " he'll be 's father ower again. *'E'd* never stand for no nonsense even when 'e were a right little 'un ; I minds the time "—but Ben had vanished. Deacon, on the subject of Bellman, his favourite hound, was apt, in the opinion of the former, to be a little tedious.

The old kennel huntsman smiled and continued to lean over the railings, recalling the exploits of Bellman the Hound, while he watched the manœuvres of Bell Boy the Puppy.

CHAPTER II

THE OLD FOX

ONE sunny morning, about the middle of November, an old red dog-fox lay out on a warm sheltered patch of grass on the moor.

It was one of those days in November when the air is soft and mellow, but with just that faintly bitter dampness in it that proclaims that in spite of the deceptive warmth, autumn, with its riot of colour, golden mornings and keen frosty nights, is really here. There was hardly a breath of wind, and the smoke from the keeper's cottage in the hollow away to the left went up in a soft, unwavering blue spiral. It was pleasant on that patch of close-bitten turf, sheltered by great clumps of gorse, and Charles James lazily stretched in luxurious contentment, and closed his narrow obliquely set eyes. He was full fed and sleepy.

The night before, the good spirit of foxes had led him to a hen cabin, the slide of which had by some

13

lucky chance been left up. When Charles James poked his sharp, questing muzzle into the small square space his eyes had shone green in the warm gloom as he listened to the faint squawks and fluttering movements of the occupants of the perches.

That night forty-five fat Leghorn pullets had retired peacefully and dutifully to bed, but the following day only thirty-two met the farmer's boy when he came with the morning feed of corn. A number of neatly severed heads told their own sad story, and the boy's mouth fell open, and his eyes rounded in dismay as his startled gaze took in the details of the old dog-fox's work of the previous night.

" Crikey ! " he muttered, picking up one of the severed heads, and regarding it with a certain mournful interest. The remaining tenants of the cabin quickly and cheerfully picked up the grain, conscious only of a larger share than usual, their interest in the scanty remains of their sisters less even than that of the boy, who picked up his measure, and with lagging steps went slowly back to face the wrath of the farmer.

Meanwhile, tucked away in his sheltered retreat, the red fox slept in the warm sunshine. He was an old veteran, whose scarred muzzle was frosty, and when his upper lip wrinkled back, it exposed yellow fangs; there was a bare patch or two on the rusty coat; his sole remaining splendour being his white-tagged brush.

As he slept off his full feed of the night before,

the day wore on, the sun climbed higher, and little sounds came up from the field at the foot of the slope the other side of the wall, a rattle of chains, the clink of a ploughshare as it struck a stone, and the voice of the ploughman calling to his team as they reached the end of the long damp furrow, and then the harsh croaking protests of a couple of big black crows, as they flapped heavily upwards, annoyed at being disturbed in their meal as they followed in the wake of the plough; and still the old red rover slept, soothed by the pleasant warmth, and sluggish after his night's gorge.

Presently another and different sound penetrated the deep sleep of Charles James. The sound that brought his head up, and cocked his sensitive ears, was one that for generations back had roused in his ancestors the fear and the instincts of self-preservation that are so deeply engrained in all foxes. Sweet and shrill it came again, piercing the still, moist air. The horn.

The big fox was on his feet now; raising his nose and tilting his head a little on one side he sniffed, his lips wrinkling; stretching each leg and arching his brush, he stood, listening, one fore-paw lifted.

And as he waited there in his prickly shelter, a new sound reached his quick pricked ears, the voices of hounds, not the deep yearning 'ough 'ough of fox-hounds, but instead, a gay ringing chorus, merry and tuneful, yet hounds just the same.

Every hair of him a-tingle, the red dog-fox stood an instant longer, statue-like, then, flattening his ears,

he turned and slid quietly down a dark prickly tunnel
of gorse, strong and rank with the smell of rabbits,
and trotting along the top of the slope, turned right-
handed into a little sheep-track and disappeared.

.   .   .   .   .

Across the stretch of burnt and blackened heather
came twenty couples of Beagles, among them, Bellman, Stormer, Bellmaid, and Brawler and Boisterous,
Bellman's two brothers. Noses down and sterns
waving cheerfully, they moved blithely through the
sharp prickly heather roots.

Ben was hunting hounds, with one of the field,
an enthusiastic young man fresh from college to
assist him as Whip—Deacon had not turned out, and
the Master was away on business.

Ben, conscious of having the ordering of things
all to himself, felt rather proud as he tramped across
the moor, in the midst of his hounds, a pleasant
sight enough in all his bravery of green and white.
But in spite of the lovely morning and his pleasure
in carrying the horn, his round jolly face was rather
gloomy, because so far they had had no luck at all,
never so much as a sniff of a hare, and not a sound
from the hounds, except when young Gossip and
Rival put up a rabbit on the edge of the moor.

Just because he had the hounds to himself to-day

Ben was doubly keen on getting a run, and with any luck a kill to finish with, so that he could show Deacon that he wasn't the only Huntsman that could show sport and kill hares. He strode on through the heather —it was higher now, nearly up to his knees—cracking his whip, that sounded on the still air like pistol shots.

The hounds spread out and pushed manfully through the thick dark heather, some of the smaller ones, such as Roguish, Paragon, and Little Prodigal went through and over it in leaps and bounds, the last-named who had, as is the way of Beagles sometimes, by some mysterious chance "bred back" to some far off "pocket" strain; but though only thirteen inches, he was showing signs of developing into such a brilliant hunter that Deacon had pleaded against drafting him for his small size, as the Master had at first decided on doing. Ben's face lengthened visibly as Hounds moved on with never a whimper, time was getting on, and not a hound had so much as feathered. When they came to a steep slope studded thickly with gorse, he directed his Whip to hurry up to the top of the hill and keep a sharp look out.

Several of the hounds showed a disposition to lie down and roll, instead of getting their noses down— another bad omen for the day's sport, thought the young huntsman as he climbed the slippery grass slope.

However, Stormer and Bellman and most of the older hounds were threading their busy way amongst the gorse bushes, and presently a white-tipped stern began to wave, and the deep throaty voice of Pirate sang out that he had found something. Mermaid, who was just behind him, confirmed the old hound's news in her light soprano, and " Hark to Pirate ! Hark, hark ! " cried Ben, hastening towards the spot; and the other hounds all ran over to Pirate, whose stern was lashing with excitement as he snuffed ecstatically at a patch of smooth, close-bitten turf; when Bellman put his nose down, a wave of warm rank scent rose up to his eagerly questing nostrils, not hare, but an intoxicating smell that made his blood tingle and race. Lifting his head he gave a long triumphant yowl, and dropping his nose down again was off down that narrow rabbit-smelling tunnel, closely followed by Stormer and the rest of the pack, every hound towling away in a gladdening chorus that warmed the cockles of Ben's heart. He himself had been down the slope, and so couldn't see what hounds were sniffing at in the little clearing amongst the gorse bushes; the young amateur Whip on higher ground saw all right, but the patch of flattened grass told him nothing, nor did the rank smell left by Charles James—he had never smelt fox in his life.

Had Deacon or even Ben been on the spot, they would have known at once that no hare had been " clapped " there, and their quick knowledgeable eyes would have noticed a tiny white feather stuck on one of the gorse prickles close by. But Deacon was at home in the kennels, boiling the meal and flesh, in readiness for the hungry hounds on their return, and in the intervals nursing one of the " young entry," who had taken a chill ; while Ben, well, Ben was racing after the flying pack with joy in his heart. Had he known that hounds were on the line of a fox, it is extremely doubtful if he would have had them whipped off just then, he was so bored with walking over the moor.

He and the Whip ran doggedly on, and for the first mile they had their work cut out to even keep the pack in sight. With that strong scent burning in their noses, hounds fairly raced, in a compact group that would have gladdened old Deacon's eyes to see, though had he known what manner of quarry they were hunting with such zest his pleasure would have quickly changed to disapproval. Every minute Ben expected hounds to swing either right or left, but never a bit of it, straight on they ran, skimming the top of a loose stone wall and into a grass field; here scent lay stronger than ever, and they fairly fled over the short green pasture, white and tan and pied bodies stretched close to the ground.

As they burst through the opposite hedge, Ben gaped in surprise. "Rum sorter 'are this," he muttered to the Whip, toiling alongside, but the young man fresh from college didn't reply, wisely saving his breath for other purposes, and he needed all that he could get. The cracking pace was telling on him, and he dropped behind Ben a little, who in harder fettle was still keeping up a fair speed; the remainder of the small " field " had been thinned out long ago, and were scattered over the countryside—small coloured dots in the distance.

The pack, still close together, was making straight across the furrows of a recently ploughed field, and the college man groaned as he vaulted heavily over the fence, and felt the sticky yellow clay cling affectionately to his thin canvas shoes. But Ben was in still worse case: he was wearing very strong heavy leather shoes, that in a very short time felt like ton weights on his feet, as he made his way diagonally across the damp furrows.

But they had to keep going, hounds were still running like smoke and with a good cry.

As Ben pushed his way through a thin, high thorn hedge and watched the pack top a rise two fields ahead, his surmise of some way back became practically a certainty—hounds were on the line of a fox; but having no desire to spoil a rattling good hunt, Ben grinned and kept his thoughts to himself.

A couple of fields ahead, Bellman and Stormer were running together as usual. They were both of them tremendously excited by this strong, strange scent that tantalised their noses so delightfully, Stormer in particular was madly keen to get on terms with the quarry, he and Bellman were leading the pack, and in their voices there was a blood-yearning high wistful note that made the young first-season hounds forget their tiredness, and gallop faster.

And three fields farther on still, a very tired old fox galloped doggedly forward. The odds were against him; he was a long way from his own country, having been scared out of his special grounds by a big shoot two days before. The fresh country bewildered him, and the heavy feed of the night before hampered his speed; the sticky wet clay wearied his feet and clogged his brush, whose gallant white tag trailed limp and mud-stained now. He was a very " old customer " indeed, and so far this season hadn't run before hounds at all, consequently he was sadly out of trim and slack. His mouth felt dry, and his tongue lolled; he had ceased to pick his route, but galloped blindly on, stark fear in his brain, instead of guile, and fear in his heart, fear all about him, as his shrinking ears heard the eager clamour of hounds' voices rising and falling, but always nearer.

His pace had slackened the last mile or two, his tired legs still carried him over the ground and the voices of the hounds sounded very near now, but his sight and hearing were becoming dim, and his brain misty; he staggered a little as he struggled on.

Crawling stiffly through a hedge, he came out into a field, at one end of which sheep were feeding in an enclosure, and the old instinct to foil his line guided him towards them. But as his faculties were failing fast he didn't see the heap of loose sheep-netting lying on the ground. Hounds poured into the field, and as they sighted the old dog-fox they redoubled their eager cry.

The red veteran, though sinking fast, had just sufficient left in him for a final effort. He sprang forward, and into the treacherous sheep-netting that closed about his tired limbs as hounds came up with him.

Wild with excitement, and their blood fairly up now, Stormer and Bellman sprang straight at their fox, that, true to his game spirit, turned and launched himself at the nearest hound. He sank those sharp yellow fangs of his deeply into Bellman's right fore-leg.

The latter let out a yelp of surprise and pain, and then closed savagely with the old rover who had levied his last toll on the poultry cabins and rabbit warrens; the pack surged over him, and long before an exhausted Ben arrived on the scene the hounds were growling and snarling round a limp, tattered body. Living royally half the year, and coming unscathed through a dozen seasons, the old red thief had at last met his appointed end; not for him the lingering agony of steel trap, nor the death by torture, dying underground like a rat, poisoned, but death in the open, time to sink his teeth in his foes, and meet his end as a gallant fox does, fighting.

Ben managed to secure the brush for old Deacon, and tossed the carcase to the small hounds, who, however, didn't tear it with their usual avidity—the old dog-fox had been a very tough and seasoned veteran.

Ben had just sufficient breath left to " blow-off " in a weak shrill fashion; then he and the weary college man collected the pack, but they were half-way back to the village where they had left the hound van before Ben noticed that Bellman was limping badly. He stopped, and when he saw the deep, angry bite he whistled.

" That joker got Bellman all right," he muttered. " Reckon old man 'ull cut up rough."

But there was nothing he could do for Bellman except go slowly, and it was a long weary tramp back to the van, and dark when they arrived at the kennels.

Old Deacon was getting quite anxious.

" I were thinkin' as ye must er lost 'ounds or summat," he said, his shrewd old eyes running over his charges as they scrambled out of the van, eager to be at the trough that was sending out such an appetising smell.

" It'd be no wonder if we'd lost 'ounds an' our-selves as well," chuckled Ben, plunging into an account of the great run.

" Fox," muttered Deacon disapprovingly, " fox, d'ye say ? "

" Ay, a right big 'un, an old dog it were," and Ben proudly produced his trophy, the rather draggled-looking white-tagged brush, which he handed to Deacon, who received it rather grudgingly, partly because he hadn't been there himself, but mainly because he didn't at any time approve of Beagles hunting fox.

As he ran his eye over the feeding hounds he

noticed Bellman limp as he moved round to his accustomed place at the corner of the trough. Stooping, he examined Bellman's fore-paw, and grunted as he saw the nasty place.

Ben watched the old kennel huntsman rather guiltily, wishing with all his heart that Charles James had set his mark on any hound other than Deacon's favourite.

" It were fox 'as did that," he explained lamely.

" I didn't reckon as 'ow a rabbit nor yet an 'are 'ad got 'old of 'is leg," dryly rejoined Deacon, as he stumped off to the special cupboard in the feeding house where he kept his first-aid appliances.

After the hounds had fed, Deacon took Bellman and thoroughly cleaned the ugly bite with a strong solution of water and boracic, afterwards applying iodine liberally, Bellman flinching at the sharp sudden sting.

As it looked a nasty place, and wishing to keep as much iodine in the bite as possible, Deacon put a bandage on, after which, thinking that Bellman would sleep better in familiar surroundings, he put him back in the kennel, in his old place next Stormer.

Poor Bellman spent a very uncomfortable night. His wounded paw burnt and throbbed, and though he tried hard to get the bandage off, he couldn't manage it—Deacon had fastened it too securely for that, foreseeing that Bellman would be certain to make a good attempt.

The moon shone into the kennel, and lit up the bench of slumbering hounds, who slept deeply, tired out after their long, strenuous day. Only Bellman was awake ; as he sat up and leaned against the wall his eyes would close sleepily, only to be jerked open again by the throbbing pain of his bitten fore-leg, the old dog-fox's last effort when he made his final gallant stand against his enemies.

CHAPTER III

A DISASTROUS HUNT

THE next morning Bellman's leg was much worse, and it had swollen above and below the bandage down to the pads of his foot.

Deacon looked worried when he took the dressings off, and Ben nervous and guilty; it was evident that the teeth of the old dog-fox had been in so bad a condition that the bite had festered almost at once.

All that day Deacon fomented Bellman's leg at intervals of half an hour; his anxiety was so great that he refused to let Ben touch it, and by night, thanks to the old man's prompt measures and unremitting care, the leg was much better, the swelling had gone down, and the matter had drained out. However, Deacon was taking no chances with his favourite, he took him down to his cottage that night, made him a comfortable bed of blankets, built up the fire, and prepared for an all-night sitting.

They looked a quaint couple, Bellman lying amidst

29

the gay red and grey blankets, wrapped in an old shirt of Deacon's to prevent the water from the fomentations wetting him, and the old kennel huntsman clad in shirt and trousers and an ancient hunting waistcoat of bright yellow. Ten years ago this "weskit" had been the pride of Deacon's heart, and he was still fond of it and wore it whenever a suitable occasion offered.

In readiness for his all-night vigil, Deacon had placed on the deal table a small shaded lamp, and a pile of back numbers of *Horse and Hound*; in addition to these preparations he had drawn a jug of beer and placed the poker in the fire, Bellman watching his movements with benevolent, sleepy interest.

As soon as the poker glowed red, Deacon withdrew it from the fire, and plunged it sizzling into the jug, by this simple method converting the beer into a sort of mulled ale, a favourite " night cap " of his.

The pair of them spent quite a comfortable night together—Deacon was always perfectly happy with a pipe and something to read, provided it related to hounds, and hunting of some kind; in fact he had gradually collected together a very useful little Hunting library, the formation of which had been largely helped on by the Master, who, at the end of each hunting season, presented the old man with a new book dealing with his favourite pastime in some form or other.

So what with his reading, and his pipe, and Bellman to attend to, Deacon passed quite a busy night.

A pretty good all-round dog vet, and never grudging the time he spent on a sick animal, Deacon generally achieved a cure, so that by the next morning the poison appeared to have left Bellman's leg, and the place looked much less inflamed.

However, for a few days Deacon kept his patient down at the cottage; doubtless the old man was secretly rather pleased to have the close companion-ship of his favourite hound, for ever since Bellman's return from the Fell Country, Deacon had seemed fonder of him than ever; and Bellman, too, was always perfectly happy in the company of the old huntsman, and when with him never fretted after the other hounds, not even Stormer.

While he was down at the cottage, the Master paid him a visit and called Bellman an " old soldier," at which Bellman from his snug bed of blankets wagged a deprecatory stern, and looked slightly shamefaced; but he cheered up immediately when old Deacon got up and lifted down a certain blue basin. Broth-time !

" By jove," exclaimed the Master, sniffing appreciatively, " I wish I was a Beagle, I do that ! " as Bellman slobbed down the savoury soup, his white-tipped stern wagging gratefully, and Deacon stood by watching, clearly delighted at Bellman's returning appetite and quick recovery.

" We shall have you out hunting again in a week or two, eh, old chap ? " went on the Master, pulling one of the invalid's long ears.

Bellman's stem wagged an eager affirmative, but old Deacon looked doubtful.

" I doan't like them deep bites wot festers," he said, " yer never knows wot mischief they leaves be'ind, even when seemin'ly the've 'ealed up nice an' clean."

" Oh, get on, you old pessimist," laughed the Master, as he gently tweaked Bellman's stern and took his departure.

For the next fortnight the leg appeared to be progressing perfectly well, but once or twice Deacon noticed, after a romp with the pups, Bellman would limp a little, and on these occasions the old man looked worried and depressed. He refused to let Bellman " turn out " even though the hound appeared to the Master and Ben to be going quite sound.

Bellman himself felt rather lonely and miserable

when the others went hunting without him, though staying behind wasn't so irksome as it otherwise might have been, because he generally had Deacon's company, and he would trot after the old kennel huntsman all day, superintending the boiling of the meat and porridge, keeping an eye on the pups, and when the weather was too bad for the younger fry to be out he would take little jaunts on his own up to the quarry.

One morning, about a month after Bellman's encounter with the fox, Deacon was at the kennels, " drawing " his hounds for the day's hunting ; though Ben hunted them it was always Deacon who decided which hounds should go, and which remain at home.

As he stood in the kennel doorway, a white coat over his green hunting kit, Bellman jumped up, and raising his head, gazed long and wistfully at his old friend, earnestly asking to be allowed to go, and as his leg had given no trouble for some time, Deacon decided he would risk it, and take him.

It was a particularly cheerful Bellman who took his accustomed place in the hound van that morning, Stormer, too, was delighted—he had missed his companion lately on hunting mornings.

The fixture for the day which marked Bellman's first appearance since his accident was at Topthwaite

—a little village about twelve miles by road from kennels, situated in rather high country, all steep slopes and thick coverts.

The morning was damp and dull, and threatened to be misty later on in the day; a raw wintery bite in the air made Deacon shiver as he stood with Ben amongst the hounds on the little green in the middle of the village. As they moved off, Topthwaite church clock struck twelve, and a pale watery sun shone out, but in a very short time it had disappeared again behind the monotonous wet grey clouds.

They "put in" at a big straggling twelve-acre field of scrubby yellowish grass, very similar in colour to a hare, and where there was generally one to be found. Sure enough, before hounds were half-way across, a big, pale-coloured Jack got up and sprang away in leaps and bounds.

Bellman's deep voice rang out joyously with the others, and the pack settled down for a run. Scent was fairly good, and for two or three fields hounds pressed the old Jack rather hard, when, finding the pack rather too close for safety, the wily veteran suddenly swung right-handed and made for a big straggling covert, a haunt of foxes, badgers, and some said of wild cats, but whether or no there was any truth or not in the existence of the last named, it was

Bellman jumped up.

certainly the worst possible place in which to lose
a hare, knee deep in bracken, in which scent never
seemed to lie, and to make matters worse, full of
rabbits.

Almost as soon as hounds got into covert there was
a rousing chorus, as a lot of the young entry opened
on the rabbits. Ben doggedly worked his way through
the thick undergrowth, and Deacon rated the impetu-
ous youngsters, but, though several of the field were
stationed at different points outside the covert, no
one saw the big, light-coloured hare quit its friendly
shelter, and there were so many rabbits about that
the chances of recovering their hare seemed very
small indeed. Deacon steadily worked his way along,
through the middle of the covert, " cracking " off
and rating the joyous excited youngsters who
were having the time of their lives amongst the
bunnies.

The moisture dripped down from the trees on to
the old man's shoulders, and the raw air seemed
to-day to be eating into his very bones. It was tiring
work getting hounds off the rabbits that kept on
popping up, and no job really for a man of Deacon's
age, but though he was no longer equal to keeping
up with the pack, he liked to be of some assistance ;
he was often there to turn hounds, and extraordinarily

quick, too, in spotting the line a hunted hare would take, but to-day he was completely nonplussed.

As he stood motionless in the thick dense covert, with the smell of dead bracken and wet earth mingling with the strong, heady, bitter-smelling larch all about him, he suddenly felt chilled through. A small rabbit jumped up inquisitively almost at his feet, but as soon as it saw Deacon it dived back into a patch of bracken, its cheeky scut flashing white, amidst the dull, wet brown stalks and curling fronds of the bracken.

A royal-blue-coated jay flew up with a harsh complaining screech, and the sudden noise tearing through the wet dripping silence seemed to rouse the old huntsman; he moved on with feet that felt suddenly leaden, but which quickened their pace as a burst of music from the other end of the covert conveyed to his unerring ear that hounds were on a hare at last. He hurried along as quickly as the rough ground would allow, but when he at last pushed his way out into the open, he was dismayed to find that a curtain of mist had gently and softly blotted out the landscape.

A faint chorus of hounds' voices—a ghostly choir —sounded away to the left, and thither Deacon turned his steps, plodding forward with dogged patience. And scudding through the chill rainy mist went the pack—strangely enough the scent was now lying not on the ground, but hanging in the air just above, so that hounds ran, heads up, and so fast that they quickly out-distanced Ben, who had been handicapped at the start by the thickness of the undergrowth back in covert.

But the hare that hounds were on now, was not the big yellow Jack, but a small dark-coloured leveret that Stormer had put up on the edge of the covert. Frightened and bewildered it quitted the safe shelter of the dense undergrowth, and ran towards a field of roots.

Before they were half-way across, a second hare that had been " clapped " there, sprang up in front of hounds, who divided, about eight couple swinging off right-handed on the line of the fresh hare, while the remainder, led by Stormer, continued to hunt the leveret.

Ben, who was some distance in the rear, heard the burst of music as hounds changed, but failed to distinguish which were on the original hare ; however, as the right-hand contingent sounded the nearest— they were as a matter of fact working back in a large circle towards him—he turned his steps in that direction, while Deacon, who, when he heard hounds go away with the leveret, took a wide left-handed cut, followed the half of the pack led by Stormer.

The root field where hounds put up the fresh hare was a large one, surrounded by a fairly high stone wall, very loosely topped. As the pack surged over this in a body, there was a sudden rattle and rumble of loose stones, and a portion of the top of the wall crashed to the ground, mingling with the scrambling, eager little hounds. A large stone pinned Bellman's injured leg, and in his sudden effort to get free, he wrenched the ligament already damaged by the punishing teeth of the old dog-fox.

He ran on, but in a few minutes was compelled to drop back, dead lame, and the pain soon brought his speed down to a hobbling trot. But scent continued to lie breast high, and Bellman followed on as quickly as his throbbing leg would let him. The voices of his mates came back to him, a little muffled through the mist, and when Bellman heard Stormer's keen high note that told they were nearing their hare, he redoubled his painful efforts to catch up with the flying pack.

The terrified leveret ran across a narrow lane, splashed in and out of a deep water-filled cart rut, pushed through the hedge on the opposite side, and oblivious to all but the dread voices so close behind, tore across the soaking grass, and plunged blindly over the edge of an old disused stone quarry, just as hounds burst through the hedge, all now throwing their tongues in joyous abandon. Stormer leading still, and going with all his accustomed dash and drive, ran straight forward on the line of the leveret, that crouched still and close, dazed with fright, on a ledge half-way down the face of the quarry.

On went Stormer, the strong sweet scent lingering and burning in his nostrils, and the wild exhilaration of it, singing in his brain, on and on—and over the edge of the quarry; and as he went his voice had a high-pitched triumphant crying note in it that went back through the mist to Bellman, and even old Deacon heard it as he plodded heavily up the lane.

When Bellman limped up he found the hounds grouped on the brink of the quarry, still giving tongue, but fitfully, as they peered over the edge into the soft swirling mist that made the quarry look like a mysterious lake; Bellman, too, peered down, and then raised his voice in a long-drawn-out howl, and Deacon when he heard it quickened his steps; directly he reached the quarry he guessed what had happened, and started at once carefully to work his way round the edge, looking for a way down.

The hounds remained at the top, giving tongue at intervals at the point where the leveret had disappeared, all except Bellman, and he followed close at Deacon's heels. When they had climbed down they found what the old kennel huntsman had

feared—no leveret, but the body of Stormer, who, in his headlong flight had crashed down on to the scattered stones below.

He was quite dead, and Deacon shook his head sadly as he knelt down and examined the limp form. Bellman sniffed anxiously at the body of his friend, and then sniffed again, whining uneasily, when poor Stormer made no response. Deacon smoothed the handsome tan head, and then got on to his feet, but almost immediately bent again, and patted Bellman.

" Come on, old chap," he muttered, " we can't do nowt no more for 'im."

Bellman licked the old man's hand, and after a backward glance or two followed Deacon, with drooping stern. As they slowly climbed up out of the quarry, Deacon shivered violently, he felt chilled to the bone; kneeling beside the dead Stormer, he had forgotten it for the time, but now the searching cold seemed to penetrate through and through. He looked down at the depressed Bellman, and pulling his ears affectionately, murmured partly to the Beagle, partly to himself :

" Now, don't you take on, lad, it were a grand way ter go ; 'e died 'untin', and 'e were close on 'is 'are at t'finish."

When they had once more reached the top and collected the shivering hounds, Deacon turned and faced the quarry, then, straightening his bent shoulders, he took out his horn and blew a long, triumphant note that echoed and rang through the mist and across the old quarry, fitting requiem to the hound that had gone to those other Hunting Grounds.

" Good sport to yer, Stormer, lad," said Deacon simply, turning up his coat collar with fingers that shook with the cold. Then with the depressed hounds at his heels he trudged off, looking through the chill white mist like some dim and ghostly huntsman of the past, attended by phantom hounds.

Occasionally a puppy would peer inquisitively round the corner of the stack.

CHAPTER IV

BELLMAN'S DREAM

THE next few days were probably the most unhappy that Bellman had ever known. Stormer's tragic death caused a tremendous blank in the life of his old friend; for five happy years they had fed, slept, exercised, and hunted together without having had a single quarrel or difference of opinion of any kind. With Stormer's going nothing was the same, and life seemed to lose all its savour for Bellman.

To add to his misery his lameness had returned, and he could only hobble painfully around on three legs, and could no longer romp with the puppies, much to the disgust of his small friends, who all rushed up to and swarmed over him, plainly asking him to come and play. But Bellman growled warningly, pushed them off, and limped away on his own, leaving behind him a little crowd of nonplussed and rather resentful pups, gazing after him, their tiny foreheads wrinkled in frowning perplexity. But Bellman was too sick at heart to heed them, and trotted slowly away, in a purposeless, aimless fashion, with no particular destination in his mind.

Disinclined even to sniff about, he pottered drearily up the field and, after wandering round, made his way to a favourite sheltered corner of his, close to a hay-stack, where on warm summer days he used sometimes to come and lie in the sunshine. Here he curled wearily round three or four times, to fall finally in a floppy heap at the foot of the stack, and heaving a deep sigh, he dropped his head on his paws and slept. He slept long and heavily, tired out by his adventures of the previous day, and the pain of his foot; occasionally a puppy would saunter up on wobbly unsteady legs and peer inquisitively round the corner of the stack, but Bellman never stirred, forgetting his miseries in the deep sleep of exhaustion.

Presently he began to dream, shifting uneasily from time to time, as his dreams gradually took shape.

They were hunting, he and Stormer all by themselves, running swiftly and easily over soft springy heather, and as they galloped, the scent rose to their happy noses, strong and warm, and made them throw their tongues joyously. They were not very far behind their hare—Bellman tingled all over, his limbs twitched excitedly, and he uttered a sharp little yap. But the "going" had suddenly changed into a wide expanse of burnt and blackened heather, charred stalks of which were sharp and prickly, and made their feet sore, but still they ran on, two solitary Beagles on the line of a stout hare, moorland bred.

Again Bellman yapped sharply, a small rabbit had sprung up under Stormer's very nose; he made a chop at it, but the cotton-tail, quick as light, plunged headlong into a clump of gorse close at hand, and neither Stormer nor Bellman bothered to follow it up, the scent of their hare was lingering too sweetly in their noses to permit of excursions after stray rabbits. Side by side they sped on, now leaping a noisy little moorland stream, now running swiftly single file along a narrow track, made smooth by the tireless feet of the little moorland sheep.

Now a great grey wall loomed up, and they had to decide whether "puss" had run alongside it, or gone over; feverishly they nosed along the wall side, their sensitive noses delicately alert to the smallest whiff of their hare. Bellman shifted restlessly in his sleep and then whimpered excitedly, Stormer had caught a tiny sniff of scent, the quarry had made a cunning swerve, and then slipped through a hole in the wall farther on.

Crying joyously, Bellman and Stormer squeezed through the narrow space; and out on to a wide rolling stretch of short wiry yellow grass, bitten close by the sheep, the scent lay well here, and they were able to gallop to their heart's delight over the short crisp grass, their long smooth ears blown back, and their voices raised in a sweet tuneful chorus. Bellman shivered with delight, and slept on, but his dream was changing; he and Stormer were no longer racing on a breast high scent, but, noses down, were working out the line slowly and painstaking. But though scent had been growing fainter for some little time now, something told them they were nearing their hare; a small object dark with sweat and with flat-laid ears was moving feebly along the wall side. The hunted hare! Bellman and Stormer fairly raced forward, in their brains a mutual thought; neck and neck they stretched over the ground, hackles up and eyes glowing red, quite near now, when—sweet and clear it came, the cry of the horn, " Come away, come away, come away," it sang.

Bellman started, yelped, and, summoned back from his joyous dream hunt, woke to the note of Ben's horn calling the hounds together as he set off for afternoon exercise.

Bellman shook himself, stretched stiffly, and after

standing at gaze a minute, watching Ben's white-coated figure move off across the field in the midst of the pack, he turned and limped towards the kennels, conscious of a sudden desire to find Deacon, a kindly comforting presence to Bellman in his loneliness.

Cheered by this thought, he hastened his steps, and trotted quite briskly into the kennel yard, but it was empty ; round to the boiler-house went Bellman, more determined than ever to find his old friend ; but though he searched all over the kennels and out-buildings, there was no sign of the old huntsman.

Bellman grew quite anxious, and even peered into the various puppy kennels, but still no Deacon appeared with his cheery smile and greeting. Feeling thoroughly depressed now, Bellman stood in the middle of the kennel yard, ears and stern drooping dismally, and his eyes worried and anxious-looking ; he had lost one friend, was the other now to be taken from him ? His oldest friend of all, who had hauled him out of his puppy scrapes, fed and looked after his comfort, and watched him kill his first hare ; Bellman did not think on these lines, but his brain was full of Deacon and queries as to where his friend could be.

He stood still, his head up sniffing anxiously, and

just at that moment he suddenly remembered the cottage where he had spent those nights when his foot was so bad, and Deacon had sat up with him and nursed him.

Full of hope, and certain now that he was on the right track, Bellman set off for the old huntsman's cottage, where he must surely be found. His foot was so sore that he could no longer put it to the ground, so there was nothing for it but to make the journey on three legs; fortunately it was not very far from the kennels, but had Bellman been forced to make the journey on two legs he would still have achieved it somehow, so determined was he to find Deacon.

When he arrived at the cottage, panting a little, it was only to find the door shut, and no sign of Deacon anywhere. It was very disappointing, and Bellman, feeling all at once very tired, sat down on the stone step outside the door. He sat there for fully half an hour patiently waiting for that inhospitable door to open, and Deacon to appear. What happened, however, was very different from what poor Bellman had fondly hoped for and expected.

When at last the cottage door did open, no Deacon appeared, but a girl—his granddaughter, who looked after the house and cooked his meals; she came out

now, carrying a heavy coal-scuttle, and was so
astonished to see Bellman sitting there that she all
but dropped it on top of him. Bellman jumped
up and wagged his stern ingratiatingly—true it
wasn't Deacon, but it was some one who could
doubtless show him where his old friend was;
so he stood on his hind legs, pawed her dress
agitatedly, and whined, asking plainly and distinctly
for Deacon; but the girl didn't answer, she only
looked down at Bellman and frowned a little as
though she didn't know quite what to do.

She looked first at the Beagle, then at the coal-
scuttle in her hand, and finally behind her into the
cottage, and Bellman, interpreting the glance, tried
to slip past her and into the house, so that he could
have a look round for Deacon himself, but the
girl was too quick for him, and making a grab
she got hold of him in the nick of time. After
thinking a minute she made up her mind, and
carrying him into the house dropped him down on
the hearth-rug with a sigh of relief—Bellman, always
a tidy weight, had not grown lighter with the passing
of the years.

However, here he was, where he wanted to be,
and there was no time to be lost. Deacon was not
in the room, but the smell of him was everywhere,

he must, therefore, be somewhere about in the house ; the girl was rummaging in a drawer—now was his chance, Bellman made a quick dart for the narrow stairs, but in the gloom he failed to notice the black cat crouched there ; and during the mêlée that followed the girl captured him again, and presently to his disgust she tied a long piece of rope round his neck, and all the time Bellman's brain centred round Deacon, puzzling over his non-appearance and wondering when he would come.

When the girl had knotted the rope securely she led Bellman out of the cottage, and shouted to a small boy who was digging in the patch of kitchen garden.

" 'Ere, George," she said, " just slip up to the kennels with this 'ound ; I can't leave gran'pa, he's that bad," and, pushing the rope into the reluctant hand of George, she ran back to the cottage.

It would be hard to say which was the more disgusted, Bellman or his small conductor, but it was certainly a very depressing journey back to the kennels for both prisoner and jailer. Bellman limped and hung back, and the little boy jerked at the rope and shouted at his charge because he didn't walk faster. It was a relief to both when they reached the kennels ; Ben was in the yard mixing the food in the

long trough, and when he saw Bellman and his small
keeper he looked very astonished.

" Where did yer pick *him* up ? " he inquired as he
untied the rope and released Bellman.

The little boy jerked a dirty thumb over his
shoulder in the direction of the cottage.

" 'E were down at t'house ; ye'd best kep 'im shut

up, we ain't no time down there to mess abart with the dogs," he added importantly.

" 'Ounds, not dogs," corrected Ben mechanically, as he stirred the porridge into the savoury broth. " 'Ow 'is the old chap ? " he inquired.

" Abart same, I reckon," replied George, taking his departure in case Ben should ask for his assistance.

George was, as he put it, " off 'ounds," regarding them as active nuisances, " wot was always wantin' summat doin'," and preferring a quiet job that could be attended to at his casual pleasure.

Bellman took his accustomed place at the trough, and gulped down a few mouthfuls of food, without much appetite ; but he would have eaten even less had he known that Deacon, his best and oldest friend, was seriously ill with a sharp attack of rheumatic fever, hastened on by his long exposure in the raw fog on their last hunting day at Topthwaite village.

CHAPTER V

PENSIONED OFF

ALTHOUGH the Master had given Ben instructions to continue treating Bellman's leg exactly as Deacon had done, there was no very lasting improvement. For a day or two it would appear to have completely mended, and Bellman would trot about on what everyone thought were four sound legs, but sure enough in a few days' time, or after a long exercise walk on a non-hunting day, the injured leg would break down again, and Ben would have to start his efforts all over again.

Doubtless one of the reasons why Bellman's leg refused to mend was because Ben was applying the treatment instead of Deacon, whose unfailing maxim in cases of the kind was " give it time." Ben, on the other hand, was young and impatient of results, and, should these be delayed for any reason, he very soon lost heart, and, in consequence, his efforts became rather haphazard. A good boy with hounds was Ben, and quite a clever huntsman in his way, but in the kennels he still had a lot to learn ; and once or twice on hunting days Bellman's leg received no treatment at all, Ben promising himself that on the day following his omission, the injury should receive double attention, and to do the boy justice it did. But these methods were of no use in Bellman's case, which required attention regularly twice a day, if the remedies were to have any lasting results.

And all this time Deacon lay ill, and Bellman in the kennels wondered and puzzled as to where his old friend had disappeared, and when he would be coming back.

Apart from his injured foot and consequent lack of his usual exercise, continual fretting for Deacon did not do Bellman any good ; he began to lose flesh and run off in condition generally, and the sight of him limping dismally about the kennel yard day after day began at last to irk the Master, so much so that he found himself seriously considering the question of getting rid of the hound. This idea of his was strengthened by the vet., who expressed his opinion that it was rather a moot point whether Bellman's leg would ever become permanently hunting sound again.

" He'll no hunt any more this season, that's a

cairtanty," he said, " though I'm no sayin' that with care he might not mend up through the summer in time for next, but then he's no sich a verra young hound, is he ? "

The Master shook his head gloomily as the vet., a rough-looking, ugly, but very kind little Scotsman, gently pulled Bellman's ears.

Had Deacon been well, there would have been no need to bother at all, the old man would have been only too delighted to take Bellman himself, but as things were, the Master shrugged his shoulders and looked very depressed. Privately, he didn't think much of Deacon's chances of recovery, and it was on this account that the Master looked so upset; he thought a great deal of Deacon personally, and, apart from this, he was well aware that in the loss of the old kennel huntsman the pack would be deprived of that which is so invaluable to hounds of any sort— care and attention in kennels, because without these a pack cannot be expected to put up much of a show in the field.

It was no wonder, then, that the Master looked sad and preoccupied; and when the vet. took his departure, leaving with Ben a lot of dressings and lotion, together with instructions for the application of same, no decision had been come to regarding Bellman's future. He had no wish to " put down " a hound that had shown himself a good performer in the field, but at the same time he was heartily tired of the sight of Bellman limping about the kennels looking as sorry for himself as if he'd lost a bone and found a biscuit; however, perhaps something would turn up, and the Master, dismissing Bellman from his mind, set off for Deacon's cottage to get the latest bulletin, which was, however, far from re-assuring—there was no change in the old huntsman's condition.

On the following Sunday " that something " for which the Master had hoped did turn up, though not quite in the way he had expected. Some friends of his came over to look at the hounds, a party of four—three men and one lady; the latter, directly Ben let the hounds out, went into ecstasies over them, and particularly so when Bellman appeared limping pathetically as he descended from the bench and came out into the yard—Ben's nursing didn't appear to be having any very good results so far. But the lady was charmed with him, game leg and all.

" Oh ! " she cried, " what a perfect love of a hound ! " and she bent down and patted and stroked Bellman so much that he began to feel quite bewildered.

He wasn't accustomed to being made such a fuss of, particularly by ladies, and he wasn't at all sure that he cared much about it either, so that when Songstress, who was always rather jealous, eagerly pushed in for her share of the petting, he quietly and thankfully slipped away, but though the lady patted and talked to Songstress, her glance followed Bellman.

As the Master watched Bellman receiving so much attention from the lady, an idea suddenly occurred to him—he was rather impulsive was the Master, and once an idea had firmly established itself in his mind, he usually acted upon it immediately. The idea that had just come into his head was this: why not offer Bellman to the lady, as she seemed so much attracted by him? Even as the thought sprang to life in his brain, a small voice seemed to ask: "But what will Deacon say?" But the Master refused to listen; Deacon was very ill and not expected to recover, and in any case Bellman belonged to him, the Master, not to Deacon, and here was a chance of getting the old hound a really good home.

As though in answer to the Master's unspoken thought, the lady said:

"I should just love to keep a Beagle, they're so quaint and charming."

She had again managed to corner the reluctant Bellman.

"No good keeping a single hound, my dear, lonely by himself; wouldn't settle without his mates."

The speaker was the lady's husband, who rarely opened his mouth, but on the few occasions when he did do so usually spoke to the point.

The Master felt rather irritated by this opinion on the part of the lady's husband, but, waiting until he and the other two men had moved away into the smaller yard to look at a litter of pups, he turned to the lady :

"Would you really care to keep a Beagle ? " he asked her, with a smile.

"Why, of course, I should simply love to have one," she said eagerly; "but why do you ask ? " she went on. "Have you got some to give away ? "

"Well, only one, to be precise," laughed the Master, "but the fact is I do want a real good home for that hound there."

He pointed casually to Bellman, and the lady gave a little scream of delight.

"But that's the very one I liked so much," she cried.

"Well, that makes it all the better, because he's the chap I want a home for," and he went on to explain the circumstances to her, and the reason he wanted Bellman out of the kennels. "You see," explained the Master, "the old chap's just lost his pal, and I very much fear poor old Deacon's number's up, otherwise I'd keep the hound on here, but he can't hunt again this season, and he just spends all his time loafing round the kennels looking as miserable as sin."

The lady listened and kept giving little exclamations of sympathy.

"Perhaps he might cheer up in fresh surroundings," she suggested; and the Master said in a loud hearty sort of way :

"Just what I think," and immediately the small voice whispered :

"You don't think that really ; you know that he'll be sure to mope more than ever by himself, away from all the people and surroundings that he knows."

But the Master again refused to listen, and so the matter was settled. Mrs. Fielding, that was the lady's name, was to have Bellman for a pet. Her husband, when he heard the news, merely shrugged his shoulders—he rarely interfered with any of his wife's plans, he had given his opinion on the keeping of single hounds, and if his wife thought otherwise, well, he shrugged his shoulders again and made his stock remark on such occasions :

" Give 'em plenty of rope." He never completed the saying, but every one knew exactly what he meant.

" When can we have the darling ? " asked the lady, rather afraid of the Master changing his mind later on, and repenting of his offer.

And " Why not now ? " genially replied the Master, and dispatched Ben to fetch some couples, put them on Bellman, and take him down to the car. Ben, secretly rather glad to be rid of his patient— he was becoming very tired of that leg—took Bellman to the big car, popped him inside, and anchored him securely to the steering wheel. Poor Bellman, dazed with the quick and very puzzling turn events had taken, hung his head out of the window and looked anxiously into Ben's face. He hardly realised as yet that he was really going ; and when Ben left him and walked back towards the kennels, he didn't try to escape, but just sat and gazed out of the open window.

Presently his new owners and their friends, accompanied by the Master, came down to the car. Mr. Fielding drove, the two men sat at the back and Mrs. Fielding in front, with Bellman crouched rather uncomfortably on her lap. The Master patted Bellman's head, more certain than ever that he had arranged things for the best.

"Be a good lad," he said. "You're going to have the time of your life I can see!"

The lady laughed. "We'll see that he has a real good time," she promised, "and he'll love playing with the other dogs, won't you, pet?"

She addressed this remark to Bellman, who, however, continued to look dubious and rather unhappy. Mr. Fielding regarded him with a kind of gloomy sympathy, and carefully reversed the car out of the kennel gates.

"Old hounds don't play; if it had been a pup now——" after which remark he relapsed into his usual silence.

CHAPTER VI

THE STRANGER IN THE CAMP

THE moment Bellman crossed the threshold of his new home he became a changed animal. The good-natured, gay, self-confident Beagle disappeared, leaving in his place a timid, anxious, and rather distrustful little dog. When Mrs. Fielding led him into the hall he followed with the utmost reluctance, and with the couples round his neck stretched to their extreme limit.

Everything about him filled him with surprise and fear; the shiny polished floor, the terrifying skin rugs scattered about—a fine jaguar pelt with the head on was particularly awe-inspiring, it had been " set up " snarling, and its gaping red mouth, fierce glassy eyes, and long white teeth filled Bellman with alarm —his claws slithered on the polished boards as he sat back on his haunches in his frantic anxiety to avoid the dangerous spotted beast.

In the end Mrs. Fielding was obliged to walk

round the jaguar instead of across him ; but hardly had this danger been safely averted than a second surprise was sprung on Bellman. As they crossed the big hall there was a sudden flurry and scamper, and a great rollicking Dalmatian pup about eight months old galloped clumsily across the hall to meet them ; while some distance in the rear, wheezing and snorting, its large prominent eyes goggling with indignation, puffed and panted a bright, golden yellow Pekingese, who the moment he caught sight of the shrinking Bellman coughed and chuff-chuffed like a small agitated train.

But Harlequin, the Dalmatian, far from being disgusted with the new arrival, was deeply interested. He had never before during his short life seen a Beagle, and in Bellman he thought he had found a new playmate, the right size, and more sensible in every way than that small magnificent egoist, Wang, who had by this time advanced right up to the dazed and bewildered Bellman. Two at once was really a little too much, and his new mistress, seeing this, pushed back the eager exuberant Harlequin until such time as Wang had concluded his fussy but leisurely investigation of the strange new dog. Satisfied at last that the Beagle was at least harmless, Wang left him and went back to the chesterfield on

Wang and Harlequin.

which he had been sleeping when Mrs. Fielding and Bellman arrived ; there, from his superior height of cushioned ease, he surveyed the latter with scorn, and barely concealed distaste.

Harlequin, after repeated efforts to induce Bellman to play, at last gave it up in despair, and also retreated to the chesterfield, and sitting down solidly on his spotted haunches, he regarded Bellman with bright questioning eyes that seemed to be asking rather quizzically exactly what the new guest was going to be good for.

The Dalmatian did not get on to the big-padded chesterfield, which was regarded by Wang as his own exclusive property ; he sat down alongside it, at intervals thumping the floor invitingly with his cheerful-looking spotted tail, but Bellman refused to be drawn by these overtures, he felt thoroughly upset and anxious. Every fresh sound startled him, and worst of all in this strange new world, there was not one single familiar or reassuring smell, all was new and puzzling to his kennel outlook.

Seeing that it was hopeless for the moment to proceed farther with the job of making the three friendly, Mrs. Fielding got up, and tethering Bellman securely to the leg of an arm-chair, she left the room after a backward glance and warning word for

Harlequin. Wang took no further notice of the new arrival, and after staring a minute or two, subsided grunting into the softness of the chesterfield, and burying his squashed nose in his plumey tail, he promptly dismissed the stranger from his mind, and with true Oriental philosophy dropped into peaceful slumber.

Harlequin, on the other hand, young and full of vitality, was spoiling for some fun and exercise; and planting his nose down on his big spotted paws, and waving his tail, he gazed entreatingly towards Bellman, and barked shrilly.

But far from showing any desire to join him, Bellman, craving only solitude and safe cover from all the horrors that surrounded him, retreated quickly under the big chair, and crouched down thankfully in the friendly gloom, his heart still going pit-a-pat.

The disappointed Dalmatian didn't know quite what to make of this manoeuvre on the part of Bellman. At first he thought it must be some new game, and pushing his pink-mottled muzzle under the chair, he yapped eager encouragement; however, as the Beagle took no notice, beyond retreating still farther into the gloom, he grew impatient of this rather one-sided game, and pushing his head right into Bellman's shelter, playfully nipped the Beagle's stern as a further inducement to come out and be sociable.

This plan, far from succeeding, had just the opposite effect on the object of Harlequin's attentions. Uttering a sharp yelp of mingled pain and fear, Bellman sprang out the other side of the chair, and in his agitation knocked over a small table loaded with various odds and ends, all of which descended on the culprit's unfortunate head.

The Dalmatian pup was delighted—here was a state of things just after his own heart. Wagging his long whip tail, he jumped about, barking loudly, while Bellman, still anchored to the leg of the chair, crouched dismally amidst the havoc he had wrought. A big bowl of chrysanthemums had overturned, and thoroughly drenched the Beagle, while the great ragged white and tawny blooms lay scattered temptingly about the floor. It was too much for Harlequin; seizing one of the largest, he eagerly tore it to pieces, strewing the petals far and wide with true puppy zeal.

The criminal himself, if such a condition were possible, was more miserable than ever; he lay and shivered, partly from fear, but principally from the effects of the cold water that had soused down on to his back when the vase had toppled off the table.

Just as Harlequin was deeply engrossed with his fifth chrysanthemum, and Bellman had sounded the utmost depths of his misery, Mrs. Fielding came in ; naturally she was rather annoyed, but as Bellman obviously could hardly be made more miserable than he already was, she couldn't be very cross with him ; so as Harlequin had been caught in the very act of dissecting a chrysanthemum, most of the blame fell on him ; however, greatly to Bellman's surprise, he didn't seem to mind at all, and the moment Mrs. Fielding stopped slapping him he pranced gaily round her, waving his spotted tail, and evidently in the best of spirits.

Presently a maid appeared, and to Bellman's relief cleared away the evidences of his crime, and when the water had been mopped up and the table put back on its legs he breathed more freely ; but after the accident he hardly dared to move about at all, and even when Mrs. Fielding released him from the leg of the arm-chair, he stayed where he was and watched Harlequin, who had taken himself over to the chesterfield to tease Wang.

The latter, thoroughly upset at being roused up out of his comfortable snooze, scowled terrifyingly and exposed two tiny white buck teeth ; but not one whit impressed by this display, the Dalmatian sprawled his big paws across Wang's recumbent form and, taking the beautiful plumey tail between his strong teeth, gave it a sharp tug. Just as Wang was working himself up into a rage, preparatory to stern measures of reprisal, the door opened and the maid came back, this time carrying a large tray.

A reassuring smell at last. For the first time since his arrival in this strange place, Bellman tilted his nose skywards and sniffed with real interest. Harlequin, too, seemed pleased, and left off teasing Wang to lollop clumsily across the hall to meet her.

After the maid had arranged the tea-tray on the table beside Mrs. Fielding she went out, and brought in a stand with shelves on which were arranged different sorts of cake. Noticing Bellman's sudden interest, Mrs. Fielding was rather pleased, and gave him a nice little cake covered with pink icing; though it tasted rather strangely to Bellman, who had never in his life eaten anything in the least like it, he bolted it, hound fashion, at a single mouthful, and then looked expectantly for the gift to be repeated. Mrs. Fielding laughed, and said :

" No, you must wait a minute ; it's the others' turn now."

Indeed Harlequin was already dragging at her arm with a large insistent paw, and Wang was seated on a hassock close by, looking the picture of injured, celestial dignity. He ate his cake very slowly, dropping crumbs on the carpet; Bellman looked wistfully at the bits of icing scattered about, but Harlequin was too quick for him. Rushing forward, he gobbled every crumb that Wang had dropped.

When Mrs. Fielding had finished her tea, the maid came in again, carrying three bowls, which Harlequin and Wang regarded with deep interest. Mrs. Fielding poured in some milk and a little tea, and dropped two lumps of sugar into each bowl, and a newspaper was spread out on the floor, on which the maid then set down the three bowls.

Wang and Harlequin bustled forward at once, but Bellman didn't move for a minute—it was a long time since he had eaten alongside other dogs, and out of a separate bowl. However, when his new mistress pushed the bowl invitingly towards him, and he saw the other two lapping away, he became more interested, and plucking up courage he dipped his muzzle cautiously into the bowl.

The three drank their tea in quite different fashion. Wang as usual fussed round and snuffed about beside his bowl before he started drinking; he always did this, and the only reason Mrs. Fielding could think of to account for this little habit of his was so that he,

Wang, should have some tea left after Harlequin had finished his.

The Dalmatian, on the other hand, had downed his allowance in the twinkling of an eye, standing with forelegs splayed, puppy fashion, swallowing in noisy gulps. He waited now, eyeing Bellman's bowl hopefully—he had no hope of getting near Wang's—the small dog was an expert guard over his own possessions. Bellman, still rather apprehensive, crouched over his bowl, and drank in hurried swallows, his eyes glancing round restlessly, ready at any fresh alarm to rush away and take cover again. However, nothing further happened, and he was able to finish his tea undisturbed, much to the disgust of the attentive Harlequin, who had evidently hoped for something different.

But Bellman was still very hungry, the small cake and the tea had filled only a tiny cavity; in fact, so hungry was he that just for the time being he quite forgot to feel so frightened of everything. As Mrs. Fielding was afraid to let Bellman loose in case he got out, and as she could no longer with safety leave him tied up, she gave him into the charge of Charles, the "Boy," and directed that he should be fed and then put to sleep with Harlequin in a small room known as the boot-room.

Bellman enjoyed his evening much better than the afternoon, for the kitchen was full of the most lovely smells, and every one was kind and friendly towards him. Very few of the servants had ever seen a Beagle before, and consequently he found himself the hero of the hour. Somehow he didn't mind these people petting him nearly as much as he had Mrs. Fielding. They had a more reassuring smell, and when they patted him they generally gave him a bit of meat or fish; it was quite pleasant, and gradually the void in Bellman's interior began to fill.

When he was feeling very full fed and drowsy from the heat of the kitchen fire, Charles, the "Boy," who had a round jolly face, and whose row of shiny buttons looked as though at any minute they might fly off, conducted him to the boot-room; in one corner there was a large round basket, in the exact centre of which lay a softly snoring black and white spotted heap, Harlequin, sunk in the sound sleep of puppydom.

Alongside Harlequin's bed was an old basket chair in which Charles had arranged a curious woollen rug, knitted in all sorts of colours; making dog rugs was Mrs. Fielding's way of finishing up odds and ends of wool, and very cosy coverings they made. Bellman found himself turning round three or four times, and then tucking up quite comfortably in the basket chair; he was too full of food to-night to start his anxious prowling, or miss his bench mates too much.

The moon shone in, and by its light Bellman, peering down through the wicker-work slats of his bed, could see Harlequin, who lay, a confused jumble of black spots, mottled nose, and pink-padded feet. Bellman sighed with relief, he was not quite alone; there was a creaking noise as the old hound wearily tucked his nose between his forepaws, and, wriggling a little deeper into the knitted rug, slept.

CHAPTER VII

BREAKFAST FOR TWO

IT is an old and well-established fact that a leopard, be he ever so desirous of doing so, cannot under any circumstances change his spots, and, were such a proceeding possible, what a tedious and painful business it would be. This changing of spots was somewhat akin to that which had been happening to Bellman during the last few days, and very tiresome and confusing he was finding it.

The process of changing a kennel dog into a house one is never a particularly easy one, but when the dog also happens to be a hound, and kennel-bred for generations back, then the task becomes more complicated and difficult of attainment than ever. For instance, he was always ready for something to eat, and whenever his unerring nose proclaimed the news of food somewhere handy, he naturally took the obvious course and ate it ; this he gradually discovered was quite wrong, and not only did he get into trouble himself over this food question, but he also led Harlequin astray as well, at least that was what Mrs. Fielding said, but Henry, the footman, when he overheard her remark, coughed behind his hand and said afterwards to Charles, the " Boy " :

" Lead that there piebald 'orror wrong ! Why, 'e were born crooked, look at 'is coat for a start."

" Look at his stummick," chuckled Charles, and they both regarded the sleeping Harlequin, whose pinkish stomach, faintly mottled and patched with blue, threatened almost to overlap his basket, so unnaturally distended was it.

" Likely 'e'll bust," hopefully suggested Charles, the " Boy," but Henry shook a gloomy head.

" Nay," he said, " one as is born to 'ang 'ull never bust."

It had happened like this. That morning, Charles, who had been detailed off to keep an eye on Bellman, had just before breakfast ceased to do so, knowing the Beagle to be quite safe with Harlequin in the boot-room. But the latter, always impatient in the mornings to be up and doing, grew tired of waiting for Charles to come and let them out; standing on his hind legs, he pawed the handle of the door with a clumsy but surprisingly efficient foot. Owing to daily onslaughts on the part of the

Dalmatian puppy, the catch of this particular door had become very loose and insecure, and on this eventful morning, in a very short time, Harlequin's pink-padded paws had achieved that to which Charles ever afterwards referred as " a bloomin' miracle."

Obligingly the door swung open, and together pied hound and spotted dog stepped jauntily out and trotted down the long, softly carpeted corridor; and as they blithely progressed, a beautiful scent was wafted to Bellman's keen nose, a scent that made him tilt his head and sniff rapturously, but which at the same time gave him a hollow sensation in the region of his stomach. Quickening his pace and still sniffing, he turned to the left, Harlequin following just behind, his puppy eyes eager, and on his odd whimsical spotted countenance a look of keen interest that gradually increased to one of lively anticipation as the delectable scent became suddenly stronger. The appetising smell did not take them very far, and the pair ran it " to earth " at the big sideboard in the dining-room.

Bellman stood up on his hind legs and sniffed and sniffed, and no wonder, because to a hungry beagle the various scents coming from that sideboard were simply demoralising.

A dish of savoury kidneys and bacon under a big

silver cover occupied one end, on another dish in the middle a brace of cold partridges sat neatly side by side, and at the far end there was a noble ham, rosy pink, and covered on the top with crisp brown crumbs. Bellman and Harlequin had the dining-room entirely to themselves, not even Wang was present—he always slept in Mrs. Fielding's room, and was not " down " yet.

There was a high-backed chair conveniently close to that wonderful sideboard, and Bellman, who, as we have said, was feeling rather hollow, sprang up, and by reaching up the back of the chair could just manage to get hold of the partridges. Making a quick grab, he clutched one safely in his jaws.

But Harlequin couldn't wait—it was beyond him to stand patiently in a lowly position while Bellman juggled with those entrancing smells up above ; he, too, jumped on to the chair and, pushing clumsily past the Beagle, shouldered him on to one side, so that Bellman, losing his balance, jerked the dish, and down came Bellman, Harlequin, and both partridges. Almost before bird number two had reached the carpet, Harlequin had secured it, and then for a short exquisite space the only sounds in the dining-room came from the jaws of the two raiders.

Never in his life had Bellman tasted anything quite

so delicious, not even during the time when he had lived with the gipsy horse-coper. The plump little birds had been kept sufficiently long to have acquired a beautiful " gamey " flavour that lingered soothingly on the palate and tongue. For the next few minutes Bellman and Harlequin were in paradise, but alas, only for a brief delectable space, because, unfortunately, partridges are only small birds, and there were but two. In five minutes not so much as a tiny bone remained, and Harlequin and Bellman were once more reconnoitring for further supplies.

The scent coming from under the big silver cover intrigued the Beagle tremendously ; he simply couldn't tear himself away—not that he had tried very hard— he just kept on pushing and shoving that annoying cover with his nose.

Meanwhile, Harlequin, with puppy simplicity, had taken the first thing he could see, and was making deep inroads into the ham. Crouching with his back towards Bellman, he was very soon happily engrossed and evidently delighted at getting this particular spoil all to himself.

The first intimation he received of the success of Bellman's efforts was a tremendous clattering crash as the big cover tilted off the dish and bounced down on to the floor. The sudden noise was terrifying, and for a few seconds even Bellman was rather appalled by the success of his efforts, but not for long—the scent of the kidneys was filling his nose with fragrance. Happily he buried his nose, and once more for a brief delightful space was transported into a wonderful elysium.

Cold roast partridge is savoury and acceptable to the majority of mortals; freshly grilled kidneys are pleasing to all save the most jaded palates. Bellman wasted no precious time in a comparison of the respective merits of the two as breakfast dishes, but just got down to it.

.   .   .   .

The sound of footsteps coming down the corridor caused Bellman to lift his dripping chops guiltily out of the dish, which, except for a small pool of fat, was now void and empty.

Equally guilty, Harlequin also glanced up agitatedly, his mottled jaws still crammed with a juicy pink mouthful. Having been more closely associated with human beings, he was the first to act. Without troubling to make use of the chair close by, he jumped clumsily off the sideboard, but, unfortunately, his large, rather long-nailed paws caught in the cloth, which slithered off the highly polished surface, bringing in its train everything that was on the sideboard, including Bellman.

The astounded Henry, just coming in behind a large tray of tea and coffee pots, etc., was so horrified that he only just saved himself from adding his quota to the varied assortment already on the floor. Making a supreme effort, he staggered to the table and set down the tray, after which he turned his attention to the crime—the criminals were no longer there; Harlequin, already an adept in the difficult art of making neat unostentatious exits, had slipped quietly away, and Bellman, on this occasion humbly relinquishing the post of leader, followed at his heels.

Harlequin, well aware of the enormity of this joint crime, sped swiftly and stealthily up the shallow, softly carpeted staircase—a terrified beagle close behind—and made straight for his favourite refuge in times of trouble—under the bed in one of the spare rooms. Panting a little, the Dalmatian hurled himself against the door, which opened immediately, and, owing to the force of Harlequin's onslaught, swung to again, very nearly catching Bellman's hindquarters.

The bed, a big double one, was hung with beautiful vallances of rose-pink silk, the splendour of which was quite lost on the two fugitives; but though he failed properly to appreciate their beauty, Bellman was more than thankful to cower down in their dim pink shelter. Once there, he licked his chops uneasily, though with a decided appreciation of the kidney flavour that still lingered pleasantly. A minute shred of ham was stuck to Harlequin's upper lip; always economical, he removed and ate it, after which the two crouched together as far under the pink canopy as they could get.

In the distance they could dimly hear their names being called, and automatically Harlequin's spotted stern thumped a response, but he didn't move, and gradually the voices grew less and less coaxing, and ever louder and more angry.

Bellman shivered, and pressed himself closer to the floor; it was a truly horrible situation for the leading hound of a well-known pack of Beagles to be in, crouching under a bed in the company of a large spotted puppy; how far removed from the safe orderly routine of the kennels. Bellman whined uneasily, and Harlequin shoved up against him in clumsy sympathy.

After a time the voices died away, and inch by cautious inch the two criminals edged up to the side of the bed and, lifting the pink canopy, peered guiltily out. The room was empty and perfectly quiet. Bellman blinked a little as he quitted the subdued pink gloom, and emerged at last into the bright sunshine. Now that the ominous voices no longer sounded in his ears, Harlequin was almost cheerful again, his whip tail wagging optimistically.

He trotted briskly to the door, anxious to be once more up and doing.

But a fresh calamity faced them here; the door, owing to the force with which Harlequin had burst it open, and on account of the draught from an open window, had most inconsiderately slammed itself to again, and they were no longer merely fugitives, but prisoners. Bellman, who was something of a philosopher and accustomed to being shut up, accepted the depressing fact quite calmly. Strolling round the room, he selected a deep arm-chair, well cushioned and padded, and curled up in its soft depths ; and presently lulled by cold partridge and grilled kidneys he fell asleep.

But Harlequin couldn't settle down and make the best of a bad job. He wandered round and round the room, whining and looking for a way out ; gradually his protests grew louder and louder, until Bellman woke up, and from his comfortable arm-chair regarded the Dalmatian in pained astonishment—*Harlequin was proving himself a quitter.*

With his mottled nose pointing to the ceiling, his large piebald ears drooping dismally, his spotted tail at half-mast, Harlequin was howling loudly, howling for help, and for some kind person to come and release him from prison. Quite soon, in fact from Bellman's point of view far, far too soon, the Dalmatian's anguished cries were heard, and they were released, but only to be led away to punishment ; certainly out of the frying-pan, but equally certainly into the fire.

.   .   .   .

That evening as Bellman lay in the old basket

chair in the boot-room, sore in body and spirit, he suddenly had an idea, almost dazzling in its stark simplicity; it was just to accomplish that which subconsciously he had been desirous of doing ever since his departure—return to the kennels. That feat once achieved, and Bellman felt in his simple faith that all would be well.

Bellman threw his tongue in a long-drawn-out wail of disappointment.

CHAPTER VIII

BACK TO THE KENNELS

THE room was very still, the only sounds being the laboured breathing of the man on the bed in the corner, and the loud hurried ticking of the big hunting watch on the table close to the bedside.

It was nine o'clock in the evening; ever since the morning old Deacon had been putting up a gallant fight against heavy odds, and now as the day dragged to a laboured close it seemed as though something of the old huntsman's game fighting spirit was dying with it. All day he had tossed from side to side, muttering and talking in his restless delirium, getting more and more excited as the fever reached its height. Deacon had always been a very strong, healthy man, never taking to his bed, but always battling along and keeping going somehow, because, like most very strong people with good constitutions, he had a horror of being ill, and going to bed always seemed to him to denote the end of things.

But this time it looked as though Deacon had taken one chance too many; the rheumatic fever had taken a strong hold, as it very often does on the strong, and, never a man who carried much flesh at any time, the old huntsman had shrunk now to a mere shadow of his former self.

He lay perfectly motionless, his thin brown leathery old face had paled to a yellowish tinge, and the far-gazing keen blue eyes had sunk back into his head, and seemed to have a misty film over them. He was fast sinking into a species of coma, and the only signs of life were the occasional restless movements of his hands, and the laboured rise and fall of the old yellow hunting "weskit" that he had insisted upon putting on when he finally took to his bed.

On a small table drawn up close to the bedside were a variety of objects—Deacon's hunting watch that the Master had given him on the memorable day when they had accounted for three hares; that was thirty years ago, when both Deacon and the Master had been young men, fine runners, and gluttons for pace, never tired, no matter how long and gruelling the day had been.

Beside the watch was the little wooden box where the old man kept a few treasured mementos of various kinds, some of them rather odd. There were, for example, a couple of hares' ears, both with little labels attached, inscribed in Deacon's thin, spidery handwriting; on one of the labels the writing had wandered up and down in a most erratic manner, trailing off at the end into a big blot. That was the label that Deacon had written out on the never-to-be-forgotten day when his favourite hound, Bellman, had been returned to him by means of that which Deacon always considered as a wonderful sort of miracle.

Many times since then had old Deacon lovingly fingered that particular hare's ear and then gone up to the kennels to gaze happily on Bellman as he slept contentedly on the bench or played with the puppies.

In the box besides the two hares' ears were a few faded rosettes won at the Peterborough and Aldershot Hound Shows, when they used to show regularly every year. Underneath the rosettes were a few photographs of favourite hounds, most of them rather blurred and faint, but perfectly clear to Deacon, who carried in his mind a distinct picture of all his old favourites. Underneath the photographs again were Deacon's special and most prized possessions—these were merely some sheets of note-paper covered with the same close-pointed writing as that on the labels.

They were remedies for various ailments; amongst them was one for the red mange, that stubborn malady to which hounds are so peculiarly prone. All day in his lucid moments Deacon had had his granddaughter going through the papers in search of a certain prescription that he wished to have tried on Bellman's injured leg. At last she found it, and it now lay by itself waiting for Ben to come and copy down the ingredients, so that he could get them for Deacon to make it—the old man never allowed his precious prescriptions to go out of his own possession. But Ben had not come, and no one had had the heart to tell the old huntsman that Bellman was no longer an inmate of the kennels.

When the chimes of the grandfather clock in the kitchen below came softly upstairs striking ten, the girl sitting by the fire got up, and going over to the bed poured out a spoonful from the medicine bottle on the table.

"Time for your medicine, Gran'pa," she said, trying to lift the old man's heavy head from the pillow.

But there was no response. Old Deacon was a long way on his last journey. He had heard the horn sound from over the hill, his eyes were half-shut, and his fingers had ceased their restless wandering over the red quilt; he lay quite still without a sign of life except for the laboured beating of the tired heart.

His granddaughter was frightened. After another fruitless effort to rouse the old man, she turned to put down the spoonful of medicine, and just at that moment the yearning cry of a single hound came through the night—a high-pitched mournful sound that made the girl start nervously.

A slight movement from the bed made her turn round. Deacon's eyes were wide open and he was muttering something, one hand moved feebly in an effort to attract her attention, she bent down:

"Yes, Gran'pa, what is it?"

"Bellman"—the words came slowly and with difficulty, but quite distinctly. "It's Bellman; 'e's shut out." The old huntsman spoke in a halting whisper. "Go an' get 'im in; Ben's likely forgot 'im, 'e's that careless."

He frowned as the girl hesitated, uncertain what to do for the best.

"Won't you take your medicine first, Gran'pa? It's long past the time," she pleaded, but Deacon moved his head on the pillow with feeble impatience.

"Go an' get the 'ound in first; it's Bellman I tell 'ee," he muttered, his voice growing stronger as she still hesitated. Again the mournful baying rang through the room, and Deacon pointed feebly to the door.

"Be sharp, my dear, 'e's wantin' ter be in," he said, moving restlessly on the bed.

His granddaughter gave in. "All right, Gran'pa, I'll go an' get back quick," she said, and turned and ran down the steep stairs. Deacon lay back again, but with an air of waiting for something, and his deeply sunken blue eyes never for a moment left the door.

Meanwhile his granddaughter was standing at the door of the cottage, gazing with beating heart through the gloom towards the kennels—she knew the sound that had roused her grandfather from that death-like stupor couldn't have been Bellman's voice, because Bellman was fifteen miles away. She listened intently, glancing up at the dark, cloudy sky fearfully, where a rather watery moon was riding high. Of course, she reflected it would likely be one of the hounds baying the moon. She went quickly into the cottage, glad to be back once more in its bright friendly warmth. As she stood for a moment in the kitchen she heard a faint cry from the room above, and sped up the stairs to find old Deacon wide awake, in his eyes an eager question.

"Well, my dear, well, did you get 'im in, eh?"

he demanded in the slightly querulous tones of a very sick man.

His granddaughter made up her mind.

"Yes, Gran'pa," she said steadily. "I've shut him in the washhouse along with Judy"—Judy was Deacon's little rough-coated white terrier.

"Ay, I'm glad o' that," said the old man simply. "Bellman was allus such a one fer a bit o' comp'ny."

He lay back contentedly, his old eyes blinking a little at the firelight; then after a few minutes he spoke again:

"Reckon I'd better take the physic, child, then I'll likely sleep for a spell."

His voice sounded much stronger, and to her astonishment he appeared to swallow the medicine without difficulty. After that he lay back and his eyes closed. His granddaughter could hardly realise the old man's surprising rally.

"Do you really feel better, Gran'pa?" she asked him anxiously.

"Ay, my dear, an' I mun see about Bellman's leg in the mornin'," he murmured, and then his tired eyelids drooped and he slept, for the first time for many nights, breathing easily and naturally.

. . . .

The moment had arrived, and with it Bellman's

great opportunity. The door of the boot-room creaked and slowly opened to admit the stout form of Henry and a reluctant, chastened-looking Harlequin. Stealthily Bellman crawled out of the old basket chair, and, slipping behind Henry, trotted out at the door and into the long dark passage, pushed open the swing door at the end, and emerged into the kitchen. So far so good. An anxious moment now. Would the other door be open? Fortune favoured the Beagle; at the door stood Mary, the cook, deep in conversation with Sandy, the gardener. As cook excitedly waved one stout red arm that still wielded a fish slice, Bellman sneaked up and pushed past her large blue print form, and out into the dark, damp shrubbery. As he crawled under a large dripping laurel bush, he heard a startled ejaculation from cook and a grunt from Sandy.

"There now, if that dratted ' beadle ' 'asn't gone now!" cried cook—she always called Beagles " beadles."

"Hoots, that's naething tae cry aboot," placidly rejoined Sandy, his mind dwelling on sundry large paw marks and deep holes adorning his cherished flower-beds. True there were no blooms at present, but as Sandy truthfully remarked, " 'Ounds are still 'ounds, mairs the peety, nae matter whether it's

December or July." He was thinking of his herbaceous borders later on when he uttered the above-mentioned profound truth.

" Better say naithing aboot it; it's too dark tae go seekin' the beastie the noo."

Comfortable council from Sandy; and as cook disliked getting her feet wet quite as much as did the big grey Tom lying before the kitchen fire, she agreed with Sandy, and they continued their discussion on matters of greater import than a mere runaway Beagle.

In the meantime Bellman was galloping happily down the long avenue; very soon now he would be out on the road. He went very quietly past the little lodge at the gates, with its one light shining out like a friendly beacon, and squeezed easily enough under the big white gate; after standing for a moment with uplifted paw, he turned and set off at a purposeful trot down the road that led to the right. He felt perfectly happy, and sniffed the chill air appreciatively; all sorts of interesting scents came drifting to his sensitive questing nose. Sometimes when the smells were particularly intriguing Bellman stepped off the road and investigated in the stiff frosty hedgerows, but more often he ignored them and trotted steadily on.

At intervals great blinding lights lit up the road

and Bellman, and cars rushed past into the darkness, leaving the Beagle quite dazed and bewildered for a minute or two, but he still kept moving forward in his dogged, purposeful way.

Once he heard a crackling rustle in the hedge and a big hare hopped out into the road, and when Bellman saw that he gave a long yowl of joy and tore after it, and when the astonished old Jack bounded indignantly up the opposite bank and burst his way through the hedge the Beagle was close behind that tantalising, bobbing scut.

The grass was short and crisp with frost, and Bellman thoroughly enjoyed his short run. He gave tongue cheerfully, and a group of shaggy young horses, the frost gleaming on their long rough coats, flung up their heads and thundered across the field, startled half out of their wits by this strange night hunt.

But very soon, just as though he had remembered something more important than hunting hares, Bellman pulled up and, making his way back to the road again, resumed his journey. Never for a moment at a loss which way to go, he turned into a narrow lane with deep frozen cart ruts, that cracked and splintered under his heavy paws. As he made his way up the long dark lane, he heard all manner of strange little noises in the hedges that towered above him on either side—stealthy rustlings and soft snappings of twigs brittle with the white frost—but Bellman turned neither to left nor right, and when he got to the top of the lane he came into a stackyard. All was silent except for a quiet munching sound that came from the covered fold yard—a thin, black cat with a crooked tail crept stealthily out from between the stacks, bent on some mysterious private quest, because night is the time when the cats come into their own. Directly she caught sight of Bellman's black, tan, and white form she spat and yowled, and disappeared into the dark passage between the straw stacks. Bellman gave a start of fright, and just then there was a rattle of a heavy chain, and a great, gaunt, yellow collie sprang on to the wall surrounding the stackyard and stood on the top, his hair standing along his back in a stiff ridge. He gave tongue in a volley of hoarse, throaty barking, but by this time Bellman was out of sight and half-way across a ploughed field. As he lolloped cheerfully across the slippery frozen furrows, he suddenly realised how thirsty he was, so when he came to a big dyke at the top of the field he scrambled down on to the thin ice that splintered in all directions, letting Bellman into the icy water with a sudden plop ; still, he managed to get a long, satisfying drink. He started on again refreshed, and was soon trotting through a quiet village. Here he was on familiar ground; there was no one about, and all the houses were shut and still, even the dogs were asleep, but for all that Bellman felt suddenly very happy. He quickened his pace and turned up a narrow dark lane by the churchyard, and, after going a little way, he forced his way through the thorn hedge, raced happily across a grass field, then another, and now familiar buildings loomed up, red roofs and iron railings—The Kennels! Bellman pushed through the yard gate and up to the kennel door with the old hare's mask nailed on it.

Here he stopped and gazed up inquiringly, but there was no sound; and the old hare, looking down at him in the pale moonlight, seemed to be mocking him, as though it knew that he was shut out. Lifting up his nose, Bellman threw his tongue in a long-drawn-out wail of disappointment; up and up it went, but the only answer was a faint rustling of straw and a muffled whine or two as his former kennel mates shifted restlessly on the close-packed benches.

Bellman shivered, and again his voice rose and fell on the chill December night   But there was no response, and Bellman rather disconsolately turned away from the inhospitable door, and made his way up the paddock to his old place, the hay-stack.   There was still half of it left, and, after turning wearily round two or three times, he flopped down and burrowed as deeply into the hay as he could. He licked the pads of his feet that the frosty ground had made a little sore, and then tucked his muzzle behind his paws with a tired grunt, conscious of a great content and feeling of well-being. His quest was finished, he was home again; presently he slept.

CHAPTER IX

BELLMAN'S NEW FRIENDS

THE following morning, to Bellman's dismay, the moment he presented himself to Ben's astonished eyes, that worthy seized him and shut him up in a small kennel by himself. It was dreadfully disappointing, and poor Bellman lay down in the straw, a very puzzled and depressed hound.

During the morning Ben brought him a large bowl of porridge and broth, with lumps of meat in it ; Bellman fell to joyously. It seemed a good long time since his last meal, which had been that wonderful breakfast of the previous morning that he had shared with Harlequin—the kennel food was not as savoury, but still it went down very well, and Bellman made no complaints. He felt a bit more cheerful after this until late in the afternoon, when he heard a well-known voice—a voice that during the last week or two Bellman had learnt to know very well, and had come to dislike exceedingly. The voice that sounded now in his shrinking, unwilling ears was the voice of Henry, the stout footman.

The next moment the lock turned, and the door swung open. Framed in the opening was Ben, and peering over his shoulder, as Bellman had feared, was Henry. His large red face was wreathed in smiles on this occasion, however, and he addressed Bellman quite good naturedly:

"Well, old chap, thought you'd give us the slip, eh? Got tired of us, I reckon."

Bellman, in hearty agreement with Henry's supposition, reckoned so too. He got on to his feet and stood looking at Henry; his stern waved uncertainly, but more decidedly as Ben called to him to come out. Directly he got outside, however, and saw the couples in Ben's hand it ceased to wave at all, and drooped dismally; when the collar was bucked round his neck, he followed Henry with a hang-dog aspect and a heavy heart. So it had all been in vain, his escape; his long journey through the night had been for nothing at all, he wasn't to stay at the kennels, and *he hadn't seen Deacon*.

At the gate stood the car used for station work, with John, the second groom, at the wheel. Henry

lit a cigarette, and scrambled cheerfully in, hauling
Bellman after him. Ben waved his hand. John
started up the car, and they were off. Bellman
hung his head out of the window, and the wind
blew comfortingly past his ears. As they passed
Deacon's cottage the Beagle could see Deacon's
granddaughter standing in the doorway, but what
was the good of that? Bellman shifted restlessly.

"Old chap's taken a turn for the better, I hear;

last night it were," remarked the footman, throwing his cigarette end out of the window, close to Bellman's nose.

"Ah, is that so? Well, I'm right pleased to 'ear that," rejoined John, and then he looked kindly down at Bellman, who sat between them now.

"Must a bin you as browt 'im a bit o' good luck last night, old feller," he said, little dreaming of just how much Bellman had all unwittingly contributed towards his old friend's sudden rally.

All at once Bellman raised his head and sniffed appreciatively; his nose had caught a pleasant scent of horses and hay, it was coming from John. Bellman dropped a heavy head across the latter's knee, sighing deeply as he did so; smells were but poor comfort after all.

"Return of the prodigal," laughed Henry, as they turned in at the lodge gates under which Bellman had squeezed so light-heartedly the night before. "But I don't reckon as Cooky 'ul 'ave killed the fatted calf for 'im or aught o' that sort; she 'ain't forgot yesterday mornin' yet, eh?" went on Henry, who seemed in a jovial mood.

"I dessay not, but we'll find 'im a bit o' summat all the same," promised John, pulling one of Bellman's long smooth ears with the soothing, knowledgeable fingers of the genuine "dog man."

Instead of pulling up at the house, John drove round to the stableyard. After he had put the car away, he conducted Bellman to the saddle-room—Henry, to the Beagle's relief, had disappeared. The saddle-room was a place after Bellman's own heart; for one thing, it conveyed instantly to his nose a pleasant reassuring message, a delightfully mingled scent of dressed leather, horse-rugs, tobacco, and men. This was a great relief to Bellman, whose nose, during his stay with Mrs. Fielding, had been constantly tormented and puzzled by the odour of flowers, perfume, and women's gear generally. He stood in the middle of the floor sniffing and gazing about him, trying to take in his new surroundings, his stern waving gently. On two sides the walls were covered with glass-fronted cupboards, lined with green baize, and filled with various kinds of bits, stirrup irons, and spurs, all gleaming like silver. A row of saddles occupied pegs one above the other, the case on the other wall was full of bridles and harness of all sorts, and in the spaces between the cupboards were photographs of famous horses, giants of the turf, whose names will never be forgotten—St. Simon, Pretty Polly, Galopin, Stockwell, Gallinule—great-hearted horses, long since passed to those other dew-spangled fields of some equine paradise, but whose spirits live on in their gallant sons and daughters, who worthuy uphold the grand traditions of their sires and dams on the short green turf of the racecourses of earth.

John put a little kettle on the fire, and then went over to a small corner cupboard, from out of which he took two big mugs, a teacup minus its handle, and an old brown teapot whose spout, like the teacup handle, was a thing of the past. Whistling softly, John next produced several big sandwiches from the pocket of a coat hanging up in the corner.

When the kettle boiled he made the tea, and going to the door shouted loudly, and presently in came a little bent old man, all twisted and gnarled with rheumatism so that his limbs resembled part of an old tree. He had a thin, foxy face criss-crossed with lines and wrinkles, and his coat sagged on his shrunken shoulders, but he had wonderfully neat little legs encased in beautifully polished calf-skin leggings. After him sauntered a short nondescript-looking youth, with a shock of dusty fair hair, and a general air of having spent the greater part of his life in the hay loft. When the little old man saw Bellman he laughed in such a queer, cracked, falsetto chuckle that the Beagle regarded him rather doubtfully, but directly the little man, whose name was Mr. Shuttleworth, and who was called the stud-groom, snapped his fingers,

Bellman walked over to him at once, and made friends.

" Got tired of yer up at 'ouse, 'ave they, old fellow ? " chuckled Mr. Shuttleworth, patting Bellman. " So ye've come ter see wot *we* can make on yer, I reckon."

Bellman sat down on his haunches, and his stern thumped once or twice, but he didn't look round, because his eyes were fixed unwaveringly upon a large piece of sandwich that John was holding up. A moment of acute suspense, and Bellman opened his jaws, and deftly caught the lump of bread and meat. This was all right, he was enjoying himself more at this tea-party than any he had had with Mrs. Fielding ; he drew a little closer to the fire, and sat himself down squarely between John and Mr. Shuttleworth.

The little stable-boy, who answered to the name of Jacky, didn't take any notice of the new arrival. Immediately upon entering the saddle-room he had taken possession of the cup without the handle and a small stool, and was now slowly and noisily absorbing the sweet hot tea while his eyes travelled absorbedly up and down the pages of a paper-backed book with the picture of a cow-boy on the cover.

" 'E's no dog man ain't Jacky, nor 'oundman

neither——" lamented John, grinning as he tossed the last bite of sandwich to an attentive Bellman.

" Well, come to that, he ain't no 'orseman neither," took up Mr. Shuttleworth, one cunning little eye fixed on Jacky's shock head bent over his book. " Blest if I know wot 'e be, but I do know wot 'e ought ter be," went on the old stud-groom solemnly.

Jacky looked up from under his thatch of hair suspiciously.

" Why, a worm o' course," resumed Mr. Shuttleworth; " you'll 'ave 'eard 'ow set on readin' worms be, bookworms they calls 'em, and our Jackie's allus got 'is nose in some book or t'other."

Bellman thumped his stern again amidst the roar of laughter that followed Mr. Shuttleworth's little joke.

The Beagle felt a bit happier now; he had had quite a few chunks of sandwich, and had licked up the sugar at the bottom of the mugs with scrupulous care—he had looked anxiously at Jacky's teacup, but the boy's finger had already done its work well and truly in that direction, much to the Beagle's disappointment.

After thoroughly exploring the saddle-room, and after he had been shown the rather mangy-looking mask of an old red fox which John took down from its nail on the wall, Bellman sank down on the strip of carpet in front of the fire, and watched his new friend wash and polish a bit and carefully soap a saddle and bridle. After that John took him down a long corridor with loose boxes leading off it, and introduced Bellman to the occupants.

First of all there was Lucifer, the big bay thoroughbred that had won a couple of point-to-points, and was therefore the pride and pet of the stable. Bellman felt very small as he stood in the box near the big horse, and he moved away quickly when Lucifer dropped his head and blew loudly through his nostrils.

In the next box was Flame, a chestnut mare, whose thin satin skin twitched, and who swished a long tail irritably when John and Bellman entered her box. When the former adjusted one of the straps on the roller that kept her rug in place, she flattened her small pointed ears, and presented her visitors with a generous display of the white of her eye.

Bellman was quite pleased to go into the next box, which was the home of Tommy-Tittle-Mouse, a grey pony who did odd jobs, and who, directly they went near him, turned round with hopeful cocked ears and lifted a plaintive fore-leg. He kept rubbing a pleading nose up and down John's coat sleeve.

" No, I ain't got nowt for yer; I ain't *made* o' carrots an' sugar, an' don't you be forgettin' it," and John slapped the fat-crested neck affectionately.

After they had looked at a large black horse, an old hunter of Mr. Fielding's that was now pensioned off, and a shy, wild-eyed, long-tailed, dark brown four-year-old, with a mealy nose, John turned to Bellman. " Now you come along 'er me," he said, pushing back the inquisitive youngster that was trying to follow them out of the box; " I'm goin' ter introduce yer to yer bed-mate." He chuckled, and led the way across the yard to another stable, a two-stall one ; one of the stalls was empty, but in the other stood a bay cob just fourteen-two. He had a bright glowing coat exactly the colour of a ripe chestnut when the sun shines on it; then he had " black points," and on his near hind foot one of the neatest little white socks you could wish to see.

When John and Bellman came in he looked round with a gay little whicker of welcome.

" Well, Taffy, lad, 'ere's yer new bed-mate," said John pleasantly, going up and patting the smooth neck.

Bellman had followed John right into the stall; and when Taffy lowered a soft, inquisitive muzzle, the Beagle put up his own nose quite fearlessly. Taffy gave a long-drawn-out snuff of inquiry, and then a little snort or two ; on the whole, he seemed pleased with Bellman.

Hitherto Tibbs, a large black cat, had shared the stall with him, but an untimely bullet from a keeper's gun had carried off his little friend, and for the last few weeks Taffy had been alone. He seemed to miss Tibbs, hence John's thought of introducing the Beagle as a possible successor.

After John had kicked the straw into an inviting yellow heap under the manger, he beckoned coaxingly to Bellman, who walked up and flopped down obediently—he was feeling a little tired now with the day's experiences, coupled with his long journey of the night before. Taffy gazed down at him with both ears sharply pricked and a sort of twinkle in his big, well-opened, intelligent eyes.

Before he left the stable John put down an enamel dish of water in case Bellman should feel thirsty during the night, then after a final twitch at Taffy's rug and a farewell pat to Bellman, he went out whistling, and shut the door.

.   .   .   .   .   .

That evening when Mr. and Mrs. Fielding sat at dinner in the big dining-room with Wang and Harlequin poised on alert haunches beside them, their

Bellman and Taffy.

noses raised expectantly. Mrs. Fielding said, " I've sent Bellman to the stables to see if he'll settle any better there. I really can't be bothered with a dog that keeps running away; I can't imagine why he didn't settle down in the house, I am sure we did everything we could to make him feel at home."

Her husband looked up and his eyes twinkled. " Well, my dear," he said slowly, " I looked in at him to-night when I went round the stables, and he looked happier and more at home in the stall with Taffy than ever he did sitting in your drawing-room—no accounting for tastes, you know," he finished with a chuckle, tossing a bit of meat into Harlequin's ever-ready, pink-lined jaws. " You know," he added, slyly, as Mrs. Fielding made no reply, " it's never a bit of good trying to teach an old dog new tricks; you want to catch 'em young for that game."

He spoke with a certain amount of fellow-feeling and knowledge, because for many years his wife had tried very hard to teach her husband various new tricks, though always without the smallest success, because Mr. Fielding shared with Bellman one particular trait—they both clung obstinately to old habits, and the things and the ways of life they knew and loved.

CHAPTER X

" TAFFY WAS A WELSHMAN "

FOR the first few hours that night Bellman slept the heavy sleep of a very tired hound. Just after the stable clock had chimed twelve, however, he awoke all in a hurry to hear a loud noise, and the rustling and scraping of the straw alongside him. For a minute before he was properly awake he felt rather startled, but when he discovered that the noise that had wakened him in such a fright was only Taffy lying down he felt so relieved that he even sniffed at the cob's nose.

" Oh, so you're still there, are you ? " said Taffy, tucking his black knees neatly under. " I thought you must be, for all you were so quiet, because the straw under me doesn't feel as thick as it usually does ; John seems to have kicked most of it under the manger for *you*."

Bellman felt rather ashamed of himself. " Well, if you'd rather come here yourself——" he suggested humbly, then he stopped, as he heard a snorting whicker of laughter through the gloom and a voice say :

" Better stay where you are, old chap ; I'm just a trifle on the big side to sleep under the manger, you know ! "

Bellman subsided into the crisp warm straw, feeling a bit foolish ; presently Taffy spoke again :

" Tibbs always slept on my back, kept it nice and warm, and himself as well ; what folks call killing two birds with one stone, though I've never seen it done yet, still, people say anything."

He mouthed a wisp of straw thoughtfully. After chewing in silence for a few minutes, " I suppose *you* wouldn't care to sleep on my back ? " he asked rather doubtfully ; " I must say I do miss that cat just in the middle of my back." He gave a snorting sigh.

Bellman felt rather nonplussed.

" I'm afraid," he said diffidently, " I should be too heavy for you, and then, you see, I'm used to sleeping in straw on a bench with hounds, and——"

" Hounds did you say ? " Taffy broke in. " Now I'm very fond of hounds, fox-hounds that is." He peered doubtfully at the Beagle. " You're rather a shrimp of a fox-hound though, ain't you ? " he asked.

"I'm not a fox-hound; I'm a Beagle and hunt hares," replied Bellman in a dignified voice.

"Oh, ah whateffer now, you'll likely be a small harrier perhaps; lots of those in my country; they're mostly white there, and some of 'em have rough coats, but what gluttons they are for hunting, all day on the great Welsh hills, and, given a chance, they'd do it all over again at night!"

As Taffy seemed to have forgotten for the moment about Bellman taking the place on his back of the deceased Tibbs, the Beagle thought it wiser to keep him talking about other things, because for one thing Bellman was very comfortable where he was, and he really hadn't the smallest desire to sleep on the cob's back—it seemed to him a most uncomfortable idea.

"You'll be from Wales, then?" he inquired conversationally, ignoring for the moment that Taffy had called him a harrier.

"You're right," Taffy replied complacently. "I'm a Welshman, born and bred in Montgomeryshire. I'm really what's called a hackney, but still I'm Welsh for all that, because, you see, I was born in Wales, but hackneys can be bred anywhere—some of the very best were bred here in Yorkshire," Taffy conceded generously.

"What is a hackney?" queried Bellman, who had

never heard the word before. " And what do they do, hunt ? " he added, because, hunting being the first and foremost thing in his life, he thought that possibly it was so in Taffy's too.

" Hunt, is it ? " snorted the cob. " No, worse luck ; I'd have liked fine to be a hunter, but it wasn't to be." He sighed ; and sweeping up another mouthful of straw, chewed it reminiscently.

" Well, but what *is* a hackney ? " again asked the Beagle.

Taffy thought a moment.

" A hackney, I suppose, in the old days was really a horse meant for use in harness on the roads and for hire, but now you hardly even see them except at shows when they are ridden and driven round and round a big grass ring, all of them corned up, and a bit above themselves, nearly hitting their noses with their knees every time they lift their forelegs."

" Do you ever go to shows, then ? " asked Bellman rather doubtfully.

" Me ! " snorted the Welshman. " I spend nearly all the summer going to shows ; I could show myself if they'd let me, I know the ropes so well now."

" What do you do at the shows ? " inquired Bellman curiously.

" The boss drives me in a little light carriage

" *The boss drives me in a little light carriage called a ' sulky.' *"

called a ' sulky,' and then John rides me in another class, and don't I just give him a shaking up. He always goes home saying that's the very last time he ever shows a hackney ' in saddle,' but, of course, by the time the next show comes round he's forgotten, and rides me again ; I toss him a foot out of the saddle at every stride," said Taffy proudly.

" But why ? " queried the mystified Bellman.

" Because my action is so good," replied Taffy promptly. " If I didn't lift my knees up to my nose when I trot I shouldn't be any good to show."

" You must lose a lot of ground doing that, I should think," ventured Bellman shrewdly.

" Ah, ha, that's just where you're wrong," chortled Taffy. " Not but what some hackneys do—the wrong sort—because they just lift their forelegs high without throwing them out; but the real ' goers,' such as the present company," said Taffy, winking in the dark, " fling their forelegs up and out, and go like greased lightning, left, right, left, right ; it's prime, if only they didn't fasten your head up so high."

" Isn't it very hard learning to be a hackney ? " questioned Bellman, who was wide awake now and quite interested.

" Yes, it was tiring at first," confessed Taffy. " I and my pals used to wear what they call ' boots ' on our feet, and an arrangement of straps and raw hide ropes attached to the 'boots' and running through a ring in our surcingles. We used to be be driven about in this—they called it 'stringing' us—and then we have to wear very very heavy iron shoes, specially made for hackneys, to make us lift our feet up high. I've won a nice few prizes up and down the country," went on Taffy, " but I should really like to have been a hunter. I'm pretty fast for my size and type, and I do love jumping."

He sighed and nibbled the wooden block at the end of his head-rope.

" There's nothing like hunting, of course," put in Bellman.

"I had a day's hunting once," remarked the Welsh cob dreamily. " When I was very young, only just broken, a boy had been sent out to exercise me, and we fell in with the hounds—I believe the boy on my back had meant to find the hounds if he could. What a day we had ; it was a wild rough sort of country, and the ground was rocky, and bad to gallop over. I bumped myself and chipped one of my knees, but we had a grand time all the same. I shall never, never forget those great, steep, heathery slopes and the sound of the rough-coated white hounds as they ran up and down the hillside and made the rocks all echo and ring with their crying as they searched for the fox.

"At last an old white hound, with only one eye and half his stern, put *his* nose down and snuffed and snuffed in the rocks, then he lifted up his head and opened his mouth and gave a deep, long-drawn-out cry that went ringing down the slope, and made all the other hounds leave what they were doing and gallop over to the old white hound, and they put *their* noses down and cried; and very soon after that," proceeded Taffy, "a bright red fox came quietly down the other side of the hill—funny thing, he didn't seem in a hurry at all, he stood quite close to me for a minute with his muzzle tilted and one fore-leg up— making up his mind which way to slide off across the heather. When he had gone, the lad on my back opened his mouth and screeched ' Tally Ho ' as loudly as ever he could, and there was a thunder of hoofs, and up came the huntsman in a great hurry, and when he blew his horn, down the slope pell-mell came all those white hounds crying and screaming as their clever noses told them exactly which way the fox had gone; it was a grand sight," and Welsh Taffy trembled a little and snorted softly. "I can see it all now," he went on; "the little red fox sneaking away, and then the hounds leaping and tum-

bling over the dark heather that stretched bleak and harsh, on and on and on until it met the sky. Just behind the hounds were the huntsman and whips in their red coats, going as hard as their horses could lay leg to the ground. We galloped for miles across that sharp, prickly heather through patches of soft, strong-smelling black bog, and across stretches of yellow grass standing in pools of black water that showered up as we splashed through. Sometimes we had to jump loose stone walls that fell down if we touched them with our hoofs ; and all the time those white hounds were screaming away in front, and we had to gallop hard, I can tell you, to keep them in sight. Often there were great lumps of sharp grey rock hidden in the heather, and after I had fallen down twice over these, we followed a farmer on an old grey horse, with a cocktail like mine, who knew exactly where to go, and how to avoid the hidden rocks and the patches of bog. He picked out all the narrow tracks that the little mountain sheep had made, and he knew all the best places to jump the moorland ditches. The man who rode him had hunted over that country for thirty years, and he kept some of the hounds. I found out afterwards they were called a trencher-fed pack, and that means," said Taffy, neatly forestalling the Beagle's question, " that they all lived at different places, some on the little farms away on the moors, and a few in the villages. Well, we killed our fox, and I wasn't the last up, I am glad to say," said the Welsh cob, " even though I was a new hand at the game. When we had all got our breath, the huntsman blew three long blasts on his horn, and then we all went down to a little village to a place they call an inn, and there they hung up the dead fox and sang songs, and the people all drank glasses of beer. They didn't give me any, I noticed," said Taffy.

Bellman listened entranced.

" Go on," he begged. " What happened then ? "

Taffy blew through his nostrils.

"Oh, my lad thought it was about time to be going home then, and so it was—it got quite dark long before we got there; and that ended my only day's hunting; and now I'm going to have a bite of hay."

Taffy raised himself on his fore-legs, got on to his feet, shook himself all over, and reached down a mouthful of hay from the well-filled rack.

"Pity you don't eat hay," he observed; "good stuff this clover, and plenty of flavour in it."

Bellman, not to be outdone, sauntered over to the enamel dish for a drink; the moon shining in at the little window lit up the stall, and Taffy in his smart blue-and-yellow rug. As Bellman lapped up the cold water, he felt all at once much happier. He stood a moment listening, but no sound came to his ears except the slow, steady munching of the Welsh cob. It was a pleasant reassuring noise; Bellman enjoyed listening to it, and long before Taffy was through his hay ration, the Beagle was fast asleep under the manger.

"Not a bad sort of a little harrier dog, whateffer," reflected Taffy, the Welshman; "but I do miss that cat to keep my back warm!"

CHAPTER XI

BELLMAN A STABLE DOG

THE next morning, when John came in to groom Taffy, Bellman lifted his head and greeted him with a friendly wag of the stern. Presently he got up out of the straw and stretched first one leg then the others in turn, but he showed no intention of rushing out, though John had purposely left the door of the stable open, in order to see just what the Beagle would do.

John was a firm believer in the theory that dogs, in common with people, seldom want to run away, provided they have every opportunity of doing so; it is the prisoner that is always seeking a way out.

" And any road," very sensibly reasoned John, as he unbuckled Taffy's roller, " if 'e wants ter go 'e'll go, an' if 'e can't manage it ter-day, then ter-morrer, an' failin' ter-morrer, then the day arter that; but go 'e will if 'e's once got the idear into 'is napper," which when you come to reason it out is common-sense, because in certain respects dogs and people are very much alike.

But apparently running away was not in Bellman's mind at the moment. After pottering about outside and sniffing the cold sharp air, that after the warmth of the stable felt very cold indeed, he came back inside to superintend with deep interest the morning toilet of Taffy, the Welshman. First of all, John brought the cob a bucket of water, which Taffy slowly absorbed in a long-drawn-out, satisfying draught. Bellman watched Taffy's silent swallowing fascinatedly. Was his new friend never going to stop? Ah, at last, Taffy lifted his wet muzzle out of the bucket and allowed a trickle of water to run out of the corner of his mouth as he stood blowing softly through his nostrils.

Suddenly forward went his neat little ears, and he neighed softly as he heard John's footsteps outside the door. Breakfast! Taffy stamped impatiently, and his short, cheeky stub of a tail twitched with impatience as John spread his corn out in the manger and damped it. After that John took off the blue rug and gay striped blanket, and picking up a handful of loose straw, rubbed Taffy all over, then he brushed him with a dandy brush, and after that banged him all over with a straw wisp, finishing him off finally with a cloth.

When he was quite finished, Taffy looked lovely; his coat glowed and shone like brown satin, and you could almost have used him for a mirror. Directly he was rugged up again, Taffy, the Welshman, glanced round at John out of the corner of his eye, and pawed the straw with a small impatient hoof; hay, he was ready now for his second course.

When the soiled straw had been taken out, and everything looked spick and span, John whistled to Bellman, who looked back towards Taffy, but the latter was deeply engrossed with his hay, and never even troubled to turn his head. Bellman next followed John to the row of boxes leading out of the corridor. The latter went into Flame's box first, but this time he left Bellman outside.

" I reckon you'd best stay t'other side the door, old feller," he said, " or 'er ladyship 'ere might take an' land yer one on the side of yer 'ead; she's like a lot more ladies, a bit touchy first thing in the mornin' ! "

So Bellman sat himself down outside in the corridor and listened to John talking and " huishing " soothingly as he groomed the irritable, thin-skinned, chestnut thoroughbred. Presently the Beagle cocked his ears and listened intently. He could hear a voice coming from the next box, a sharp complaining voice, not a bit like John's cheery, brisk tones.

" Nar then," it said, " stand still, carn't yer, an' let a body get on wi' t'job."

After this there was silence for a short time, and then the voice sounded again, this time shrill with pain:

" 'Ere, get orf me toe, yer clumsy little blather-skite."

The door of the box was a little way open ; deeply intrigued, Bellman pushed himself through, and sur-veyed the occupants with an air of tolerant interest.

Tommy-Tittle-Mouse stood across the corner of his box with his stout dappled quarters jammed up against the wall. Wedged between the manger and the pony's stout side was Jacky, the stable-lad. His fair dusty hair was all at sixes and sevens, wisps of it stood up on end, and a long lock lay damply across his moist forehead. His face was red, and little drops of sweat adorned his snub nose. Tommy-Tittle-Mouse, on the other hand, looked calm and unperturbed. He stood placidly mouthing hay, but his long thick tail was tucked down obstinately between his fat hindquarters, and one small iron-shod hoof was planted firmly on the boot toe of his long-suffering attendant.

" *Will* yer stand over, yer gert, clumsy brute ! "
cried Jacky, bringing down the dandy brush on the

Jacky, the stable-boy.

sleek fat side of Tommy-Tittle-Mouse with a hard
thump.

The grey pony looked round, and, catching
Bellman's eye, he seemed to wink. Then he
swung round with a little jump, and as Jacky
stooped and brushed under the pony's belly,
Tommy-Tittle-Mouse turned his stout neck and made

a quick grab at the patch on the seat of Jacky's breeches, but this time Jacky was ready for him, and planted a smart blow on the grey's velvety nose. Tommy-Tittle-Mouse reared indignantly, but after that stood still, looking the picture of injured innocence, while Jacky finished him off.

As all seemed peaceful once more, Bellman ventured farther into the box, and went up alongside Tommy-Tittle-Mouse, who eyed the Beagle with good-natured contempt; but when Bellman sniffed curiously at one of his neat yellow bandages, Tommy swivelled an eye that showed a bit more white than it should, and at the same time lifted a stout hind-leg tentatively. Bellman drew back—he had evidently made a mistake.

" I really can't stand having my bandages smelt so early in the morning," grunted the grey pony crossly, " and that silly little chump has put 'em on wrong again—all come unwound when we go out, you see if they don't ; drat these stable-boys, all alike, no—hi, don't pull my roller up so tight, boy ! " he grunted loudly as Jacky gave the surcingle that encircled Tommy's stout body a sharp tug.

" I'll soon stop his little tricks," snorted the grey pony; and just before Jacky could slip the strap through the buckle, Tommy-Tittle-Mouse puffed himself out so much that Jacky finally gave it up in disgust, and left the surcingle in the last hole of all.

"Ha! done him one that time," chuckled Tommy, at once relaxing himself, so that his roller hung in a slack loop. This little victory seemed to put the pony in a better humour, because, as Bellman followed Jacky out of the stable, he winked at the Beagle quite good-naturedly.

As Bellman trotted across the stable-yard a few minutes later intent on a little private investigation on his own account, he heard his name called, and the voice seemed to come from the direction of the saddle-room. Bellman had enjoyed himself on the previous afternoon, so he turned now, and made his way there as quickly as he could, to find John and the stable-boy busy dealing with a sort of late or second breakfast. Always a trifle peckish in the mornings, Bellman needed no second invitation. Plumping himself squarely down beside John's chair, he raised his head expectantly, ready for any stray bits that might come his way.

"I did 'ear last night," remarked Jacky, his voice coming rather muffled through a large mouthful of bread and bacon, "as 'ow old Deacon were pickin' up summat wonderful."

"Ay, 'e'll likely pull through now, I shouldn't

wonder; some o' they thinnish old chaps is as 'ard an' tough as 'ickory wood, can't kill 'em; but I reckon," went on John, " as 'e'll be a bit upset like when 'e finds as Bellman 'ere 'as come to us."

" Ah, well, 'e's a sight more just like 'im in t'kennels," placidly rejoined Jacky, to whom one dog was exactly like another, and none of any vast importance.

" Nay, that's just wheer ye're out in yer reckonin', I'm afeared, as'ow the 'ole bloomin' pack wean't make up to Deacon fer losin' this'n; he fair thought the world 'an all of this 'ound."

John sighed and gently tweaked one of the Beagle's ears. Bellman was sitting gazing into the fire through half-shut eyes, his forelegs spread wide apart. He looked as though his thoughts were far away. As John continued to pull his ears soothingly, his eyes closed, his head drooped, and his fore-paws slid farther and farther forward, until presently he stretched himself full length on the shabby bit of carpet in front of the fire, and dropped his muzzle across John's instep with a deep sigh. He slept there cosily for a little while, but woke up soon to hear John say briskly, " Well, lads, time to be movin'; I reckon them 'osses weant take their sens out."

Bellman jumped up, and stood wagging an eager stern. What was going to happen now? He watched John take down a saddle and a couple of light snaffle bridles, following closely at his heels as he went into Lucifer's box and stripped the big horse of his top rug, arranging the striped blanket tidily under the saddle. After this he did the same with the rugs of the irritable chestnut mare, only he didn't put a saddle on her.

When all was ready John led out Lucifer into the yard, and there was Jacky perched on the back of Tommy-Tittle-Mouse, and leading—yes, Bellman took a quick step forward, it *was* Taffy, looking very smart in his yellow and red striped blanket, one dainty black foot pawing the gravel, and his cheeky stub of a tail twitching with impatience.

John swung up on to Lucifer, and Mr. Shuttleworth, whose little face this morning looked all blue and pinched, led out Flame, who never had to be kept standing, and handed the rein to John.

They were off. Bellman tore excitedly down the drive, the sound of four sets of iron-shod hoofs clattering loudly in his ears. The lodge-keeper's wife ran out to open the gates, and they all trotted out into the road.

What fun it was; Bellman hadn't done anything so

pleasant for a long, long time. He lolloped gaily along the grass at the roadside, taking each little cut dyke as it came in his stride. John grinned as he watched the Beagle, "'*E's* suited, any road," he said; "steady, mare," he added, as Flame put in a little waltz step and jump—an invention of her own.

After they had been going for a couple of miles, John pulled up and turned into a narrow lane with high hedges on either side. As they swung into the lane Tommy-Tittle-Mouse snorted loudly—he seemed rather pleased about something. Bellman took up his position behind Taffy, but took care to keep out of range of the high-stepping black heels.

There was a thick white rime coating the hedges, where the sun had not been able to penetrate, and thin crackling ice roofed the deep ruts, which splintered and snapped under the trotting feet. A thick covert went along one side of the lane for a short distance, and, just as they clattered past, Bellman heard a loud whir of wings and a keen high kuk, kuk, kuk! and a fine cock-pheasant flew up in all his russet glory. John gave a shout, and Flame snorted and plunged excitely, not because she was really frightened, but more as though, being so very sensitive and highly bred, it was the proper thing to do. Tommy-Tittle-Mouse and Taffy whickered rudely, and the latter lifted his quarters in a funny little buck of amusement.

At the other end of the lane they came to a gate that led into their own park, and here, as the sun had melted the white frost off the grass, they had a short canter. Bellman had to gallop faster now. He tore

after the horses just as once he had led the flying pack on a hot scent, his ears blew back, and he carried his white-tipped stern straight out behind him. He had no time to stop and look at anything, so he hardly noticed the little group of rough-coated Shetland ponies that were running out in the park. As they cantered past, the Shelties lifted knowing heads, and stood at gaze, their eyes gleaming mischievously from under their tangled forelocks, while their long matted tails swept the ground.

By the time they reached the avenue, Bellman's tongue was lolling out like a long pink ribbon, but all the same he felt happy and his stern waved gaily.

After he had seen the horses put in and fed, the Beagle retired to the saddle-room, and flopped down by the fire, glad to stretch out after his two hours' hard exercise. He raised his head once to look contentedly round the saddle-room—the smell of leather, horse-clothing, and hay filled his nostrils soothingly.

He sank back again with a sleepy grunt. The Beagle, now a stable dog, began to snore softly, and the old fox's mask from its nail on the wall grinned down at him sardonically.

CHAPTER XII

BELLMAN'S NARROW ESCAPE

ONE morning, about a month after Bellman had taken up his quarters in the stables, he was sitting peacefully in Taffy's stall having a quiet chat with the little Welshman, when he suddenly heard his name called. Two people were calling him. One was John, but the other—just for a minute the Beagle wrinkled his tan eyebrows in perplexity, but only for a very short time was he in doubt —the other voice undoubtedly belonged to Mrs. Fielding.

As the stable door was shut, Bellman could not go and find out what they wanted, so he sat down philosophically in the straw alongside the little Welsh cob, who was always glad of the company of the Beagle. But Bellman was not to be left in peace for very long; the voices came nearer and nearer, and presently Bellman heard John's voice again.

"I reckon we'll find 'im with Taffy, Mum," it

said; "they seem to 'ave a powerful lot to say to one another, do 'im an' Taffy."

There was the sound of Mrs. Fielding laughing, and then:

"There, what did I tell yer, Mum? 'Ere 'e is, the rascal," from John, as he opened the door.

Taffy looked round with hopeful cocked ears and his usual whicker of welcome, but Bellman merely sat under the manger, looking "dogged," and thumped a rather apathetic stern at intervals. He was not particularly pleased to see Mrs. Fielding; never having been used to ladies, he was always ill at ease with them. They generally "fussed" him too much, and somehow or other always contrived to make him feel anxious and uncomfortable. Certainly Mrs. Fielding had been very kind to him in her own way, but the pity of it was that it was a way that the Beagle couldn't understand at all, and towards all that he couldn't understand Bellman showed a profound mistrust. So all the time that the Beagle lived with Mrs. Fielding they never, to quote John, "got square" with one another.

Consequently this morning Bellman wore his usual expression, in Mrs. Fielding's presence, of mild obstinacy; and quite obviously those slow, unwilling thumps of his stern were a concession to good manners—nothing else. And as usual Mrs. Fielding went up to him, instead of waiting for the Beagle to come to her, and patted and hugged him, and said what a " lovely boy " he was, and all the time Bellman stood a rigid figure of stolid endurance.

After a few minutes Mrs. Fielding got up, and to Bellman's horror produced a collar and lead, which she proceeded to buckle round his shrinking neck.

" Goin' ter take 'im for a walk, Mum ? " inquired John, smoothing Taffy's sleek quarters with the palms of his hands—it was one of his ways of getting a shine on a horse's coat. " Becos, p'raps, if you was ter take 'im int' park 'e'd foller all right—'e likes going in the park, don't yer, old feller ? " and John gently tweaked Bellman's drooping stern.

The Beagle looked round at him pleadingly. Mrs. Fielding laughed. " No," she said, " I've got a better treat in store for him than just a walk. I'm going to take him to the meet to see all his old friends—the Beagles are at Stonygap to-day—won't that be lovely, Bellman ? "

John went on absently smoothing the Welsh cob's quarters. He was a man of very lively imagination where animals were concerned, and, as is often the case when brought up against a person altogether devoid of " animal sense," he didn't quite know what to say.

" But won't that make 'im a bit 'ome-sick like, Mum, just when 'e's started ter settle down ? " he ventured at last.

" Oh, *no*," cried Mrs. Fielding, " it will cheer him up beautifully, and I want the Master to see how well he's looking. Come, Bellman, we mustn't be late for the meet, old boy, *that* would never do "; and Mrs. Fielding walked out of the stable, followed by a very puzzled and uneasy Beagle.

John sighed a little as he watched the drooping black, tan, and white form disappear round the corner of the stable-yard.

" Eh, it do seem a pity as fowks can't put they-selves in other fowk's minds," he lamented, as he straightened the cob's rugs.

Taffy glanced round with a tentative snort. " Oh, ay, I know wot's in *your* mind—oats."

John walked across to the bin, got a double handful of crushed oats, and offered them to Taffy, who licked them up in a trice.

" There, that's all this journey," said John firmly, as he slapped the shining flank and left the stable.

" I'm afeared as Bellman 'ull be frettin' ter be with 'is mates ; it's like showin' a bloke a glass o' beer an' then drinkin' it yerself," John addressed his remark to Mr. Shuttleworth a couple of hours later as they

took off Tommy-Tittle-Mouse's thick stubby growth
of mane.

The old stud-groom smiled as he ran the clippers
delicately between the grey pony's twitching ears.

" Women," he said, " never sees farther than their
noses; they're like an 'oss in blinkers, they see just
wot's in front of 'em and nowt much else, but you
wait, Bellman 'ull larn 'er a thing or two before the
day's out, I reckon, or I don't know 'ounds."

He chuckled in his high-pitched falsetto way, and
dusted the loose hair off Tommy-Tittle-Mouse.

.   .   .   .

Meanwhile Mrs. Fielding, Bellman, and the
chauffeur were making their way to Stonygap.
Bellman sat on the seat beside Mrs Fielding, stiffly
erect, gazing stonily in front of him. He still wore
the collar and leash; the collar had once been the
property of Harlequin, and was gaily decorated with
large shining brass studs, it also flaunted a medallion
that informed the world at large of the interesting
fact that Harlequin belonged to the order of Tail-
Waggers, but somehow the part didn't fit the present
wearer of the collar.

Bellman looked at this moment anything but a
Tail-Wagger; he had been dragged away from the
stable-yard and all his friends there, he was not fond

of motoring, and, on top of all, the unaccustomed collar and leash " irked " him. Every now and again Mrs. Fielding spoke to him and patted his head, but Bellman made little response to these kindly overtures, he just glanced round at her, and his stern made a slight tentative movement or two, after which he resumed his stolid gaze of dogged endurance. As they drove into Stonygap, and drew up near the village green, Bellman suddenly leaned towards the window, his ears lifted eagerly, and his stern began to wave to and fro.

There, grouped on the grass, were all his old kennel mates, and in the middle of them the Master and Ben, in their smart green kit, faced with orange, and spotless white breeches, but it was on the pack that Bellman's eager gaze was riveted.

He whined excitedly, and Mrs. Fielding smiled and let down the window as the Master came up to the car, looking rather surprised as he caught sight of the Beagle. After he had greeted Mrs. Fielding, he turned to Bellman and patted him.

" Well," he remarked gaily, " you don't look any the worse for your change, old man. How has he settled ? " he asked, with a tinge of anxiety in his voice.

Mrs. Fielding frowned a little and then laughed.

" Well, he wouldn't settle at all in the house with us," she said, " but now he's gone to live in the stables, and he seems quite happy there."

" Oh, that's good," exclaimed the Master heartily. " I knew he'd be all right," he added, lifting his cap and moving away to rejoin the pack and Ben.

Bellman looked after him wistfully, and there was a great yearning in his eyes. He pawed agitatedly at the car door until Mrs. Fielding, in desperation, lifted him back on to the seat beside her. He looked a different hound from the listless, bored-looking animal of an hour ago. His eyes shone, and he sat keenly alert, sniffing anxiously. When the Master blew his usual short note as they moved off, Bellman sprang off the seat and hurled himself at the door, whining frantically. Wilson, the chauffeur, made a grab at the leash, and Mrs. Fielding hauled him back on to the seat once more.

" I knew he'd be interested," she said, " but I didn't think he would be *quite* so excited."

" Dogs 'as wonderful long memories, Mum," murmured Wilson, with a sympathetic glance in Bellman's direction. " Shall we follow on, Mum ? " he added; " they're goin' ter put in at the top side o' the moor as usual."

" Yes, I think we might go on for a little while,"

said Mrs. Fielding, settling herself comfortably back in the car.

Bellman, on the other hand, sat poised alertly on the extreme edge of the seat, his head tilted eagerly, and every now and then a tremor of excitement ran down his rigid fore-legs ; he had forgotten all about his present surroundings and the other two occupants of the car ; his mind was centred on the hounds, and his brain teemed with exciting memories.

Presently the cry of hounds who have struck the line of a hare came back to them, and as Bellman heard the eager yearning notes his eyes glowed and he stiffened to an even keener attention. Wilson drew in to the side of the rough moorland road and pulled the car up, and they all listened intently. Again the voices of hounds sounded, a triumphant burst of joyous music that came nearer and nearer.

Five minutes later a tawny hare with flat-laid ears jumped on to the wall top and crossed the road in quick bounds. Hardly had " puss " disappeared under the wire fence at the opposite side of the road, when there was a rattle of stones, and over poured the pack, a tumbling wave of black, tan, white, and badger pye, every voice raised in jubilant thanksgiving and triumph as each questing nose owned the line.

It was a pretty sight, and Mrs. Fielding and Wilson watched entranced. The third occupant of the car also watched, but not for very long. All at once he raised his voice and poured out all his excitement and longing in a loud thrilling cry; then he gave a spring, and before Mrs. Fielding or Wilson could snatch the trailing leash, Bellman was

out of the window and squeezing under the wire fence.

How he screamed as he tore after his former kennel mates. Faintly the wind carried the agitated voices of Mrs. Fielding and the chauffeur to his ears; but what cared Bellman? His heart sang, his blood tingled and raced, and the soft, damp breeze lifted his back-flung ears as he galloped across the crisp, springy heather.

146

He had caught up with the racing pack now, and found himself galloping alongside a lemon-and-white hound, Old Challenger it was, but there was no time for greetings, not with that lovely scent rising warm and satisfying to their sensitive noses.

The heather grew high and thick on this part of the moor, and the little hounds made their way through in leaps and bounds; scent was still strong, and Bellman felt completely happy. Just in front of him galloped Bellmaid, his sister, her light soprano voice ringing out tunefully above all the others.

As they plunged under a wire fence, Bellman felt a sharp tug at his neck as the trailing leash was caught by one of his mates pressing close up alongside as they pushed and jostled their way under the tangling wire. However, as Clinker went on in front, the taut leash slackened, and Bellman ran gaily on again.

Their hare was giving them a capital run, but now puss swung sharply right-handed as though suddenly conscious that she was in strange country, and was anxious to get back on to familiar ground. And round swung the pack, and raced towards a high stone wall; a foot in front of it were a row of stout wooden posts strung with rusty barbed wire

Over went the leaders and after them all the others, struggling up under the wire.

Bellman, when it came to his turn, made a good spring, and gained the top of the wall easily enough ; but just as he crouched for the downward leap he was conscious of a sudden wrench at his neck—the leash had caught in the wire strung between the posts.

He scrambled and half-fell down the wall, choking and strangling at the end of the lead. It was a horrid moment. Desperately Bellman scrambled and struggled to get a footing between the stones, and all the time he felt his breath getting shorter and shorter. He gave a strangled yelp ; and just as he seemed at the last gasp, and his frenzied struggles were growing weak and feeble, there was the sound of heavy running feet, and a rough voice said :

" Well, dang me, if this don't beat all ; one o' they little 'ounds 'ung up in a collar."

As he spoke, the farmer lifted Bellman up by the scuff of his neck with one hand, and with the other he undid the leash that was tightly twisted in the wire.

" Nay, lad," he admonished Bellman, who crouched at his feet utterly exhausted, " yon's no way ter go 'untin', not wi' a string round thi neck, or ther'l be 'angin' of this'n for sure." He stooped and picked up the lead, and with a very dejected Bellman at his heels, he started to walk back across the moor towards the road.

As they went they kept meeting members of the field, who all glanced curiously at poor Bellman, who crept shamefacedly along as though he knew that a Beagle on a lead was a most deplorable and ridiculous sight. Just before they reached the road they saw coming towards them a hot and red-faced Wilson; Bellman wagged an apathetic stern as the chauffeur approached.

" Is 'e yourn ? " queried the farmer, jerking a thumb at the Beagle; " becos ye all but lost 'im, mate. When I come up 'e were abart at far end ; 'ung up by this 'ere strap, 'e were on t'side o' t'wall yonder," and he pointed vaguely across the heather.

Wilson was quite upset as he listened to the story of Bellman's narrow escape, and he handed the farmer half a crown when he took the lead from him.

" The Mistress 'ull be very grateful. There'd a been a nice set-out if we'd a lost this 'ound, not but wot 'e's bin a sight o' bother one way and t'other," went on Wilson, smiling broadly as the various incidents of Bellman's short but sensational career up at the house passed through his mind.

"Well, wot I allus says," replied the farmer, as he turned on his heel, "is this 'ere: everythin' is all richt in its proper place, but 'ounds out o' a pack is

like playin' cards wot's got scattered abart by theirsens, nobbut a blamed nuisance."

Wilson chuckled and looked down at the drooping Bellman.

"Now, you 'ear that, lad. Come on, we'd best be gettin' back to the car."

Bellman trotted obediently at the chauffeur's heels. The voices of his mates had long since died away; he could no longer smell that glorious hot, warm, rank scent of hare, and his neck felt sore and chafed. He climbed slowly and stiffly back into the car.

When she heard Wilson's story, Mrs. Fielding was horrified.

" How dreadful, poor dog ! " she cried ; " and how perfectly awful if the Master had come up and found the poor darling hung up by the neck, after he had been kind enough to give me the pet."

Wilson agreed, though he smiled a little as he recollected the story of Bellman's departure from the kennels, and the Master's openly expressed relief at finding a home for the old hound.

" I think we'd better go home now, Wilson ; it's getting late, and I'm sure Bellman for one has had quite enough." Mrs. Fielding handed the chauffeur half a crown, and smiled as she looked down at Bellman.

He was coiled up tightly, nose to stern, on the thick rug on the floor of the car, fast asleep. He didn't wake up until they drove into the stable-yard, and Mrs. Fielding handed him over to John, with instructions to give him a good feed.

" Yes, Mum, I've got it 'ere waitin' of 'im in the

saddle-room," replied the faithful John, escorting Bellman to his belated dinner, which, thanks to the groom, was a particularly good one.

Later on Mr. Shuttleworth and John enjoyed a quiet cigarette before the saddle-room fire, and Bellman snored steadily from his place on the old hearth-rug between the two chairs.   Said John :

" It were a narrow escape 'e 'ad ter-day 'ung up on that theer wall."

" Ay," murmured the old stud-groom, " I reckons as it taught the Mistress summat too ; but still it don't seem 'ardly fair as Bellman 'ad to be three parts 'anged afore she'd see as 'ounds aint like ordinary dogs ! "

CHAPTER XIII

OLD FRIENDS AGAIN

FOR the next six months Bellman continued to live in the stables, and he was, on the whole, fairly contented.

The hunting drew to a close. The last meet of the hare-hunting season took place on a rough, boisterous day in March, and a travelling fox gave hounds a long, gruelling run on a warm, gleamy day in April for their last outing.

The horses were " roughed off," first one rug then the other were removed, washed, and put away, ready for next autumn. Gradually the gloss left the horses' coats, as the oats ration was replaced by hay, and grooming ceased ; all except in Taffy's case, and, as he was going to be shown, they kept his coat sleek and shining. It seemed a pity for the little Welsh cob that he should not be going out to grass with the other horses, but from Bellman's point of view it was rather fortunate, because he continued to have

Taffy's companionship. The nights would have been very lonely without the Welsh cob, and particularly so to the Beagle, who, being a hound, was used to and fond of plenty of company.

Occasionally Harlequin would put in an appearance in the stable-yard, but at first Bellman hardly knew whether to be pleased to see him, or the reverse. The Dalmatian was by this time about full grown; and though just as fond of play as ever, he was now a big heavy dog, and his methods of fun were rather rough. His idea of a good game was to roll the Beagle over and over, and then tumble on top of him, a form of amusement which, while affording Harlequin exquisite pleasure, caused Bellman only acute discomfort.

Sometimes, however, they would have little trips into the park, and for these Bellman was always ready. Once out in the park, they each enjoyed themselves after their own particular fashion. Harlequin would proceed to gallop round and round in dizzy circles, leaping madly over clumps of grass and bracken, and barking loudly; after a few minutes of this he would tear round the little Shetland ponies trying to stampede them. For the first few times he was successful, but very soon the ponies grew accustomed to him, and would merely lift their noses out of the grass and stand watching with tolerant amusement the crazy gyrations of the big spotted dog, while even the tiny foals soon ceased to have any fear of Harlequin, sometimes joining in the games themselves. Bellman's idea of enjoyment was quite different; directly they reached the park he always trotted steadily over to a big patch of gorse and bramble, which he would work methodically, nose down,

pushing through the bracken until only the waving white tip of his stern was visible over the curling green fronds.

In a little while his stern would begin to lash excitedly, going faster and faster as surmise became certainty. A note or two in his deep musical voice, and suddenly out would pop a bright-eyed bunny to streak across the grass, its white scut flashing agitatedly, followed by Bellman a long way behind, giving tongue gaily in true Beagle fashion. The rabbits always escaped, but Bellman, never tired of working that particular patch of undergrowth, thinking, perhaps, that some day he would come upon that careless little rabbit that all dogs hope for.

It was very pleasant pottering about in the park, and Bellman and Harlequin thoroughly enjoyed their little outings. After the Beagle's daily hunt was over and Harlequin had tired of his crazy galloping, the pair would forgather once more, and flop down happily on a sun-warmed patch of turf, two pink ribbons of tongue lolling, eyes half closed, occasionally snapping at a too venturesome fly.

At midday they would wander back—Bellman to the saddle-room and Harlequin kitchenwards—he had become a great favourite with the cook, who was always very pleased and proud when she was occasionally allowed to take the Dalmatian for a walk, and she always had some tit-bit waiting for Harlequin, who never failed to put in an appearance at some time during the day. Later on his waist-line would begin to suffer, but at present all was well, his sleek black-and-white shape continued to look lithe and graceful in spite of the delicious illicit snacks in the kitchen.

As the summer advanced the weather became very warm, so much so that for the first time in his life

Bellman suffered from the heat. He had not grown any thinner while living in the stables; always a strong hound with rather heavy bone, he had thickened out somewhat the last few months. He missed the long runs which had previously kept him hard and light of flesh, and always in good trim. He still continued to accompany John when he took Taffy out for exercise, and the former, seeing the effect the heat was having on Bellman, would go slowly, only walking and slow trotting, a procedure that suited both the Beagle and the little hackney equally well, to say nothing of John himself, who thoroughly enjoyed the leisurely rides through the warm air heavy with all the varied scents of summer.

Sometimes when the day was very hot he shut Bellman up and made him stay at home, but this made the Beagle so unhappy that at last kind-hearted John gave it up and allowed Bellman always to accompany him and Taffy on their daily exercise rides. But when the day looked like being very hot they would set off early in the morning while the air was cool and fresh, and everything smelt new and clean, and was still cold after the chill-scented freshness of the night before. Bellman came to love these early morning runs, and would stretch out eagerly and gallop over the soaking dew-drenched turf with all his old zest. He and Taffy left dark wet trails where the grass grew long and thick, and the little Welsh cob appeared to enjoy the short spins quite as much as did Bellman.

But as the days grew longer and warmer, Bellman came to feel the heat more, and often at night, although John left the window and the top half of the stable door open, he would lie on the straw under the manger panting quickly; at intervals through the night changing his position restlessly, and going often for a drink to the big tin bowl that John always filled every night before he left. This went on until one very warm day in the middle of August.

John had gone away early to fetch home a new horse, and in his absence Jacky had been instructed to take Taffy out for his two hours' exercise.

" An' take it steady, mind," admonished Mr. Shuttleworth. " It's very 'ot ter-day, an' it's goin' ter be a lot 'otter afore it's cooler, and see as you don't tire the 'ound out keepin' 'im at full stretch; it's no sorter weather fer old 'uns like you an' me ter be runnin' about, eh, old feller ? " finished Mr. Shuttleworth.

Bellman wagged his stern politely, but kept his gaze fixed steadfastly on Taffy and the stable-boy.

They set off, and for the first couple of miles

Jacky followed out the old stud-groom's injunctions.
He jog-trotted and walked the cob, but the sun
poured down on them, and very soon Bellman's
tongue was hanging out of his mouth, and he began
to feel heavy and unlike himself. As they came out
of a long grassy lane on to the high road, Jacky's
sharp eyes noted the broad grass verge at one side of
the road. He was very tired of walking and slow

trotting, and Taffy, with his nose set stablewards and
pleasant visions of oats rising before his mind's eye,
needed no urging. In obedience to the pressure of
Jacky's knees, he broke into a sharp trot, but the
swinging, high-actioned step was too much for even
Jacky's hardy internal organs; he felt, as he afterwards
described it, as if all his " inside had come unstuck
and would presently be jolted up out of his mouth,"
so he kicked Taffy in the ribs, and immediately the
little Welshman jumped into his quick, easy canter.

Bellman stretched out at once into a gallop, but, try as he would, he couldn't keep up with Taffy this morning, his legs felt leaden and his breath came in quick hard pants. Very soon Taffy was out of sight —Jacky, thoroughly enjoying his canter, forgot all about the Beagle toiling along in the rear, and never once looked back.

Taffy, hard and fit, in show fettle, and consuming his twelve pounds of oats a day, was enjoying the canter too, and, snatching hard at the snaffle bit, the canter very soon became a sharp gallop. Half a mile behind, Bellman was in a poor way, staggering a bit now, and all the blood in his body seemed to be surging through his head—he could hardly see. At intervals he kept throwing his head up in an effort to get air, and a little foam gathered round his mouth.

All at once the green grass and the sky turned dark, he gave a choking gasp, and dropped like a stone. His limbs went first rigid and then jerked spasmodically, his jaws ground together, and the froth, pink tinged where he had bitten his tongue, looked like soapy lather. The blood filled his eyes, and he looked a dying hound as he lay with twitching limbs in the bright hot August sunshine. Flies buzzed about his unheeding form, and a butterfly or two darted aimlessly to and fro.

He had lain there for some little time, and the flies were settling round his eyes, when there was the sound of heavy wheels on the road and the steady, purposeful clop of a cart-horse. Bellman heard nothing, but presently the horse was pulled up, and a man got heavily down off the cart and came up on to the grass. He looked down curiously at Bellman, and then he gave a startled ejaculation:

"Whoy, bless my soul if it ain't the very 'ound as I walked meself, dang me if it ain't—wot's up wi' ye?"

But Bellman couldn't tell the old friend of his puppy days that. The farmer stooped down, peered at the blood-injected eyes and the froth round the clenched jaws, felt the rigid limbs, and then stood up.

"'E ain't dead; I reckon 'e's in one o' they fits or summat."

He bent again and, lifting the Beagle in his arms, carried him over to the cart and laid him gently down on the straw at the bottom. Then he pushed his old straw hat back and scratched his head.

"Can't leave 'im theer to mak' fly meat on, that's sartin sure, but wheer shall I take 'un?"

He gazed absently down at Bellman as though in search of inspiration, and after a minute he smiled and climbed slowly on to the cart.

" Oive got it," he said ; " coom up, lass, wer's got an extry journey ter mak' now."

He addressed the bay mare, who moved slowly forward, one ear back as though not quite in agreement with the farmer's project and the prospect of an extra journey. They turned up a side road, and after they had been going along here for a short distance they came to a deep, narrow lane into which the farmer turned the bay mare. As they moved slowly and with much creaking of the heavy wheels up the narrow track, the thick bushes growing on the banks at either side almost met over the farmer's head. It was much cooler here in the shady lane, and the farmer, looking down, saw Bellman raise his head feebly.

" Comin' to, are yer, old chap ? I'll lay yer don't remember me, but I calls you ter mind orl right, an' the way yer used ter chase my poor 'ens round ! " The farmer chuckled, and Bellman wagged a languid stern ; he still felt dazed and strange.

Presently the lane opened out into a piece of moorland on which grew great clumps of gorse, whose sharp prickles were hidden now by masses of glowing golden bloom. A little way on the left was a thick covert, a snug sanctuary for foxes, where a vixen could rear her cubs in peace and at the same time pick up plenty of good living from the rabbits that flourished on the moor and in the covert itself. Facing the covert, and sheltered on one side by a huge clump of gorse, stood a long low cottage, with

a strip of garden closely wired in to stop the trespassing of mischievous cotton-tails.

The farmer pulled up at the gate, and slowly and laboriously descended to the ground. Directly his back was turned the bay mare shook herself until all the harness rattled, stretched out her neck, and fell to cropping the sweet-brier rose tree that was trained along the garden fence.

Meanwhile the farmer tramped up the path, and a brace of Beagle pups that had been dozing in the hot sunshine shambled on to their feet, and lolloped clumsily up to him, wagging cheerful, friendly sterns. They waited hopefully while he knocked at the door—their main interest in life being to get into the house. In less than a minute the door opened, and there stood old Deacon, looking a bit thinner after his long illness, but still with the same brown leathery, wrinkled face, and merry twinkle as of old.

"Mornin', Deacon," said the farmer. "Oive picked up an old friend o' yourn wot was a bit over-done wi' t'eat like, an' I thout as 'e'd be better fer a glass o' water, so oive browt 'im on."

The farmer's face was perfectly grave, and Deacon looked quite concerned.

"Yer did right—'oo be it, where is 'e?" queried the old huntsman.

"'E's out yonder settin' in my cart," replied the farmer, jerking a backward thumb towards the farm cart and its silent occupant.

Deacon looked rather surprised.

"I doan't see no one," he said, screwing up his old eyes and looking hard at what seemed to all intents and purposes an empty cart.

"Nay, 'e were that bad I made 'im lie down on

t'floor ; we'd best be goin' out to 'im, or my old mare 'ull 'ave polished off all yer rose tree else.''

He turned as he spoke, and walked heavily down the path, followed by Deacon, whose thin, wrinkled face was a mixture of concern and mystification—the two Beagle pups had seized what seemed to them a splendid opportunity, and disappeared into the cottage. Slowly, and with sundry grunts, the farmer let down the back of the cart and beckoned to Deacon. " Theer 'e be," he said simply, and then stood on one side and watched the old huntsman.

" It's Bellman ! " Deacon's voice sounded thin and cracked as he almost shouted the words, and then he bent over his old favourite, his face all puckered. Bellman staggered on to his feet at the sound of the well-remembered voice, and, placing a heavy paw on each of Deacon's shoulders, he proceeded to lick his old friend's face with an ecstatic tongue, whining joyously as he did so.

Deacon lifted him out of the cart as carefully as he would have handled a baby—he didn't set him down, but walked slowly up the garden path still carrying his precious burden.

" Hi ! wot are yer goin' ter do wi' 'im ? " shouted the farmer, whose presence the old huntsman seemed to have entirely forgotten.

"Look arter 'im," was Deacon's brief reply as he disappeared into the cottage.

The farmer watched, a broad smile breaking over his big, red face.

"Well," he muttered, "oive 'eard summat abart two bin company an' three's bin a crowd; I reckon this be one o' they toimes!"

He chuckled, and laying his hand on the bridle he drew the reluctant bay mare away from the tempting sweet-brier. Climbing laboriously into the cart, he drove slowly down the rough lane, the wheels bumping and creaking over the deep ruts, and the bay mare still mouthing with leisurely enjoyment a long trailing piece of Deacon's rose-bush.

CHAPTER XIV

THE EXCHANGE

THAT evening Deacon wrote a letter that took him exactly two hours to complete to his satisfaction.

He sat at the table in the kitchen, surrounded by sheets of notepaper, which were his first attempts at the all-important letter upon which so much depended. He wore his old yellow hunting waistcoat, and he had rolled up his shirt sleeves, the better to tackle the job in hand. From the depths of a basket chair Bellman regarded him with dreamy contentment, while just outside the two Beagle pups, "Frolic" and "Fanciful," sprawled and tumbled on the grass. Tucked away in a basket under the old oak dresser was Judy, the little, rough-coated, white terrier bitch, who was busy conducting some intimate researches on her own small important person.

The only sounds in the kitchen were the slow, halting scratching of the old huntsman's pen, and the small succulent noises which marked the progress of Judy's toilet. Every time—and they were many—that Deacon paused for a word, his eye dwelt on Bellman; the sight of the Beagle's benevolent tan countenance with its familiar white blaze seemed to assist the old man materially in the composition of that very difficult letter. By the time it was finished, Bellman's head had dropped on to his paws, and the two Beagle pups had retired to bed, tired out after their play. With a deep sigh Deacon laid down his pen, and leaned back in his chair to read over the letter which was addressed to Mr. Fielding. It was as follows:

DEAR SIR,—The hound, Bellman, was brought to my cottage this mornin' in a fit, brought on, I take it, by gallopin' in the heat of the day. 'E 'as, I am glad to say, pulled round now, and will, I think an' 'ope, do all right, if looked well after. Now, sir, I bred this 'ound myself, an' know 'im from nose to stern, and I love 'im the same way. This bein' so, I takes the liberty of askin' if the 'ound might be allowed to end 'is days here with me instead of in your stables. 'E, the 'ound, is gettin' on in years like meself, and two old 'uns can look better arter one another than one can.

If so be as you an' your lady feels as you can

168

spare the 'ound, would you and her be pleased to take in 'is place a tarrier pup out of my bitch "Judy"? She is a real game sort, an the pup I 'ave in mind for you is all white, barin' a black patch over one eye, an' he looks like makin' the goods.

'Opin' you'll forgive the liberty, the pup's name is "Bitters," but me an' Bellman 'ave been pals from the start, an' I 'ave a fancy fer 'im an' me ter finish the run tergether.—Yours respectfully,

J. Deacon.

The following morning Deacon, Bellman, the two Beagle pups, and Judy all went down the lane and on to the road to post the letter, and after that there was nothing for Deacon to do but wait anxiously for a reply.

Bellman, of course, had no anxiety; he was blissfully happy in his present surroundings, there was such a lot to do, see, and smell—and he had found Deacon. The Beagle pups that Deacon was " walking," Frolic and Fanciful, were delighted to have Bellman's company, and trotted clumsily after the old hound on all his little excursions. Hitherto they had not taken much interest in the rabbits, but now that Bellman was here to " show them the ropes " and " put up " a rabbit or two for them, they grew quite keen and soon began to use their noses for themselves. The moor was a happy hunting ground for the trio ; they would set off, the two pups under Bellman's guidance working the gorse bushes and clumps of heather like steady, old, third-season hounds, raising their shrill little voices tunefully when the inevitable bunny " broke covert," and tearing in pursuit as fast as their rather wobbly legs would allow.

Sometimes they were joined by Judy, who, now that her pups were growing up, was always glad of an excuse to leave them for an hour or two. The little terrier bitch was a great asset on the " hunts," because, no matter how sharp and prickly was the gorse or bramble patch, it had no terrors for Judy, who would plunge boldly in where the Beagles refused to go, consequently many more rabbits were bolted and sport became quite brisk.

But much as he enjoyed the little rabbit hunts, what Bellman liked most of all were the long rambles with Deacon and Judy. These walks were leisurely enough for Bellman to investigate to his heart's content every tree root, bush, and tuft of grass, in which researches he was busily assisted by Judy.

Old Deacon would lean on a gate for minutes together smoking contentedly and gazing over the country with knowledgeable, kindly eyes that missed nothing, whether flower, animal, or bird, or, if they were in the fox covert, he would sit down on a fallen tree-trunk and watch Bellman and Judy's investigations with a tolerant twinkle. On one occasion the little terrier bitch caught a mole, but Bellman was not greatly interested in Judy's " kill"; he sniffed dubiously at the tiny, black, velvet-coated creature with its long, pathetic-looking pink snout.

He couldn't understand Judy's joy and triumph at all, but backed away quickly as she crouched snarling over her prize, her little dirt-encrusted, red-rimmed eyes glinting viciously. But though Bellman was perfectly happy and untroubled, the old huntsman felt worried and anxious. Four days had gone by, and he had received no word respecting Bellman's fate. The next day he stood as usual, anxiously looking out for the postman, when sure enough there he was, tramping up the narrow lane, looking warm and tired. But directly he caught sight of Deacon he smiled broadly and waved a post card.

" It's orl right, yer can keep 'im ! " he shouted cheerfully.

A great load seemed to be lifted from Deacon's mind, and he stepped down to meet the postman, looking, as the latter afterwards described it, as though " 'e'd shuffled off ten year all in a minute." He almost snatched the card from the old postman's hand, and his own trembled a little as he held it up to read. There were only a few lines of writing on it, but they told the old ex-huntsman that for which he had been longing and hoping.

On the card were the following words, scrawled in Mr. Fielding's careless, untidy handwriting :

" Keep the hound by all means, he's in his proper place now ; glad to have a pup out of the little bitch ; send as soon as you like."

His face all aglow, Deacon turned to the postman, who stood mopping his own face after his long, weary trudge up the lane.

" 'Ave you time for a cooler, mate ? " he suggested.

"No, by rights I ain't," replied the postman, "but I'll make it all the same, and thank ye kindly, Mr. Deacon."

The old man hurried into the cottage, stuck the precious card up in a conspicuous place on the mantelshelf, and went into a little stone-floored pantry for a jug of beer; this, with a couple of glasses, he carried out to the waiting postman, and together they drank:

"Long life to Bellman."

"Ye think a lot of 'im, don't yer?" said the postman, handing over his empty glass with a sigh of mingled satisfaction and regret as he glanced over to where Bellman lay on the warm flags, blinking sleepily.

"Ay," replied Deacon simply, "'e's easy the best 'ound I've ever seen, an' I've seed a few good 'uns in me time, but 'e's a 'eap more'n that ter me, 'e's just like a bit o' meself some'ow, I couldn't rightly tell yer for why, but theer it be."

"Ay," the postman nodded sympathetically. "Dogs grows into sorter 'abits, some folks 'as the same feelin' abart cats an' canary birds, meself I keeps a few 'ens. If I sets up an' 'abit, might as well 'ave one with a bit o' proffit abart it, that's 'ow I figured it out—'ens means eggs an' eggs means money. Well, so long, I'll be gettin' along now," and the postman adjusted his letter-bag and stumped off down the path.

Deacon watched him with a little smile on his face.

" 'Ens, cats, canary birds," he murmured contemptuously ; " who'd make 'abits o' them things when they could 'ave 'ounds ? "

He turned and went into a small workshop at the back of the cottage, and all that morning he was busy sawing and hammering. By midday he had made a very neat box, with a lid that screwed on. There were large round holes in the front and sides of the box, and a small square in the lid was cut out and covered with strong, fine wire-netting. When it was quite finished Deacon half filled the box with straw. Bellman watched the proceedings curiously as though half fearful lest he should be the one destined to travel in the box, while Frolic and Fanciful chewed light-heartedly the odds and ends of wood lying about on the floor.

That night, instead of three terrier puppies there were only two—the twin of Bitters (who was called Gin) and little Nettle were there, but Bitters had disappeared. Judy was not particularly upset about it ; at the beginning the pups had been a source of great interest and pride, but as they grew bigger and rougher she became rather tired of them, and her

thoughts turned once more to other matters : dark,
damp earths rank with the warm, strong taint of fox
and badger ; and great, grey rats that squealed and
bit back if given time.

Judy's white hackles rose stiffly, her eyes shone
green in the gloom, and her scarred upper lip lifted
slightly as she cocked her small ragged ears to a faint
but unmistakable sound of scratching.

CHAPTER XV

THE SHOW

THE first Saturday in September was always marked on Deacon's calendar with a large cross. It was the day on which the annual Agricultural Show was held, and during the last twenty years Deacon had never once missed " Show Day." It was an outing for the old huntsman, and he always what he called " togged up " a bit on these occasions.

On this particular Saturday he wore his best yellow waistcoat, a clean white cotton stock, and drab cord breeches ; a pair of ancient but well-cut box-cloth leggings completed a rather taking whole, faintly reminiscent of a more leisurely and picturesque age, when t'squire was t'squire and t'parson could " cross " a country with the best, and looked equally at home on his cock-tailed nag as in the pulpit.

Judy always accompanied Deacon to the show, and the question that came up now was what to do with Bellman ? Deacon pondered over the problem, scratching his head in a puzzled manner ; he didn't want to shut the old hound up by himself all day, neither did he want to leave him with the puppies, who, now they were at the " rough and tumble " age, would probably annoy and tire the older hound.

But Bellman had his own ideas on the subject; sitting squarely down in front of his old friend, he thumped an emphatic stern at short intervals, and fixed Deacon with such a beseeching and unwavering stare that the old man could no longer ignore the unspoken but none the less eloquent demand.

" Take me, too," entreated Bellman's eyes, ears, and stern, and, of course, they won the day. The three set off about ten o'clock, and reached the show-ground shortly after eleven. Judy, who had seen it all before, was inclined to be a little bored, but to the Beagle everything was new and interesting, even though a little awe-inspiring; never before had he seen so many animals grouped together.

Deacon first of all visited the cattle—as a young man he had once had thoughts of being a farmer, but that was before he had caught the hunting fever— and he still had a lively interest in farming and stock generally. As they went round the cattle, Bellman pressed close to Deacon, but Judy was quite un-troubled, and to show her careless bravado she actually walked up to a large Friesian cow lying down, clad in an immaculate white sheet, and gave the beautiful creamy tassel at the end of her tail a sharp tug. The large black-and-white lady looked round with an indignant toss of her head, and Judy pranced

gaily back, her short, cheeky little stern at an impudent angle, and her tiny, dark eyes twinkling with mischief.

Deacon hadn't noticed this little incident. He was standing, leaning on his stick, wrapped in admiration of an enormous Friesian bull, whose ebony and drip white coat shone and gleamed like black and cream satin, even his horns and hoods had been beautifully polished, and at the end of *his* tail was a

178

truly magnificent snowy tassel that immediately caught Judy's eye, but, just as she was sidling up for a closer investigation, Deacon called her back, and administered a warning tap of his stick.

" Showin' off, that's wot you're doin'," he remarked reprovingly. " You've more cheek an' conceit of yerself in yer bit of a tail than that there bull 'as in the 'ole of 'imself ! "

When they had thoroughly inspected the cattle, they passed on to the shire horses, and here Bellman was more impressed than ever ; never in his life had he seen such enormous awe-inspiring creatures. The man in charge of a great, dapple-grey stallion was busy putting the final touches to his huge charge—cleaning the " feather " on the enormous legs with sawdust, and polishing up bridle and chain.

" Ye've a grand sort there, Jack," remarked Deacon, who knew the big " shire " and his owner very well.

" Ay, I reckon we'll be up at t'front ter-day, but still, yer never knows at this game, it's a rum job showin' at toimes," replied Jack, spitting on the brass studs with vigour.

" It is an' all," chuckled Deacon, strolling on.

After a bit he stopped to light his pipe, and looked down at Bellman, who seemed more sure of himself now; his stern was up again, and he was glancing about taking a keen interest in all the varied sights and sounds going on around him.

"Ye're just beginnin' ter take wot's called an intelligent interest, ain't yer, old feller?" remarked Deacon, pulling one of the long, smooth ears affectionately. "Not like madam there; she thinks the 'ole outfit 'as bin got up special for 'er benefit, an' the rest on us is 'ere just on sufferance like," and Deacon chuckled.

The little terrier bitch was walking along, head and tail at a more than usually jaunty angle, in a cock-sure, swaggering manner that made several people stop and smile at her.

They next inspected the pigs and the sheep, neither of which pleased Bellman at all. Sheep he had always disliked, and for pigs he cherished a sneaking fear—they always startled him with their sudden, deep, menacing grunts. He was quite relieved when Deacon turned his steps towards the refreshment tent. Bellman followed the old man into the close gloom that smelt of all sorts of things, and was full of men all trying to get served first; but it would have been better for the Beagle if he had waited outside, and after he had twice had his paws trodden on, and a man had tripped and spilt a glass of beer over him,

Bellman thought so too. But he cheered up when Deacon at last emerged out of the cheerful, perspiring crowd, carrying a large paper bag and a bottle of beer.

Round at the back of the tent they found a nice sheltered corner for their picnic. Bellman was frankly delighted; he always loved " outings " that were connected with food. He stood now with gently wagging stern, his chops drooling slightly as Deacon opened the paper bag and, taking out three savoury-smelling meat pies, laid them out on the grass in a neat row. After that he opened his old black-handled hunting knife and cut up two of the pies into small pieces.

" There, get on wi' it," he said, wiping his knife on the grass, and taking a long satisfying pull at the bottle of beer.

Meanwhile Judy and Bellman " got on " with their respective pies; but long before Judy had finished sorting out the bits of meat in hers, Bellman was sitting alongside Deacon and watching with pathetic envy the old man disposing of his own pie.

" Crust seems a bit 'ard," grunted Deacon, " must a bin made to travel by post; could go all round the world I shouldn't wonder wi'out breckin'," he added, handing the last bit to the attentive Bellman, who, when he saw that there was nothing more to be had from Deacon, turned his attention to Judy, who was still gnawing delicately the odd bits of crust, and pushing them about with a slightly contemptuous nose. But when Bellman offered his help she bristled up at once, standing guard over the fragments of the feast and snarling crossly. "Now, ain't that just like a woman?" grunted Deacon, puffing lazily at his pipe; "never wants aught until other fowks takes a fancy to it, an' then yer can't get it away from 'er for the life in yer."

Bellman, defeated of his purpose, came over and flopped down beside Deacon with a deep sigh of disappointment, leaving Judy to sit over the remnants of her meat pie. She sat gazing into the distance in what appeared to be a careless, "don't care" manner; but let Bellman so much as get on to his feet, and in a second she was all abristle again.

"Well," Deacon slowly got up and knocked his pipe out on his boot, "if we don't be movin', folks, we shan't see nowt."

As they made their way towards the main judging ring they passed close by the rails where some horses were tied up. Suddenly Bellman stopped and then went up to the rails, to a bright bay cob who had a white sheet on; one small neat hoof pawed the ground restlessly, and his cheeky stub of a tail twitched with impatience.

It was Taffy, and directly he saw Bellman he lowered his corky little head and snorted loudly. Bellman was delighted, his stern wagged, and he kept giving little whines of pleasure. He was just going to start turning round and round in the inviting-looking heap of green clover in front of Taffy, preparatory to a comfortable "sit down," when the latter blew through his nostrils :

"Hi ! young fellow-me-lad, that's my dinner when you've done with it—not a bed ! "

Bellman drew back quite shamefacedly, and in response to a call from Deacon turned to go.

"See you in the ring later," whickered Taffy good-naturedly, as the Beagle rejoined Deacon and Judy.

But another pleasant surprise was in store for Bellman, because, just as they were moving away, who should stroll up but John, looking very smart in new drab cord breeches and brown leggings.

"Hello, hello, hello," he said, when he caught sight of Bellman, " been havin' a crack with Taffy, have yer ? and how d'ye think 'e's lookin', just right ter win a prize, eh ? " he laughed and patted the Beagle. " Bellman an' 'im used ter share the same

stall," John explained, jerking a thumb towards the Welsh cob.

"Oh, that's it, is it? I couldn't rightly make out why 'e seemed so friendly like, 'e's not generally that set on 'osses," replied Deacon, chuckling.

"We don't 'alf miss 'im in t'saddle-room; it ain't the same place at all," grumbled John.

"Well, your loss is my gain," said the old huntsman genially, "that's way o' t'world, I reckons; but we'll 'ave ter be gettin' on if we're goin' ter get a good place on t'stand for Bellman ter see 'is pal tak' t'red ribbon."

"Ay, that's right," rejoined John, picking up a

rubber preparatory to putting a final gloss on Taffy. " I think little chap 'ull give some on 'em summat ter go on wi' ter-day."

Taffy glanced round with flattened ears; he was getting rather tired of all this grooming and polishing business. Meanwhile Deacon and his two companions had made their way over to the grand stand and found a good seat close to the rails. Bellman was glad to lie down, and for a time curled up quietly, while Judy sat alert and keen, snapping at the flies. It was very pleasant lying there on the grass in the shade at Deacon's feet, and blinking idly at the various classes.

First there were the hunters, that made Bellman flinch and blink as they thundered past the stand at a gallop, their coats gleaming in the bright sunlight —brown satin, black satin, chestnuts dappled and shining. Bellman's head drooped again as he watched the bright horses moving over the green grass. A little later Deacon nudged him gently in the ribs.

" Wake up, old lad, 'ere's yer pal," he whispered, and Bellman sat up with a start, in time to see Taffy trotting by, head high, and neat black knees nearly hitting his nose at every stride; he scarcely seemed to touch the grass, so lightly and airily did his small hoofs go up, out, and down again. On his back sat John, his face absorbed and grave, giving no indications of the rough ride the little hackney was giving him.

He watched the judges, and reined Taffy in at exactly the right moment, and brought him to a quivering stand at the top of the row. There were seven other hackney ponies in the class, but none of them equalled Taffy in either appearance or action, and twenty minutes later John trotted past the grand stand with the coveted red card held firmly in his mouth, and Taffy flinging his legs higher than ever. As the latter passed Bellman, he turned his head slightly and seemed to wink, as much as to say :

" There now, you see, whateffer I've won again ! "

Bellman gazed after the bright bay form until he couldn't see it any longer, after which he flopped down once more at Deacon's feet with a deep sigh. They stayed until after the jumping, which lasted for an hour and a half. Just opposite them was the water jump, and whenever an unlucky competitor jumped short and soused in with a mighty splash, Judy gave shrill barks of joyous laughter—these little incidents seemed to afford her greater pleasure than anything else in the show.

Before starting for home they called in at the Old

Bell—Deacon dearly loved a chat and a drink after the show. Bellman and Judy retired under the old oak settle, and curled up there, the former to lie blinking sleepily amidst the mingled sound of men's voices, the ring of coins, and cheerful clink of glasses.

Presently, lulled by the heavy atmosphere, he slept, but Judy continued to lie awake, her sharp little eyes fixed on Deacon's boots in case he got up to go and forgot to tell her.

"Well, wot did yer think to t'show?" asked Deacon, addressing an old man who sat in the corner near the fireplace.

"Nay," replied the other, "I didn't reckon nowt to it, it's not wot it were i' my toime, shows were shows when I wor a nipper."

It was the answer Deacon had expected, and he smiled as he raised his glass.

"Ay, an' beer's a bit different now, eh, Mr. Bates?" he said slyly.

"Beer," scoffed the old man in the corner, "this stuff ain't beer, it's nobbut Adam's wine wi' a pinch o' sugar an' malt in it. "Everythin's changed," he rumbled on, "and nowt fer the better." He slammed down the mug with a heavy thud.

"Ay, not even this'n," grunted the shepherd, with a wink at the rest of the company.

Amidst chuckles of mirth Deacon got up to go.

" Theer's some things 'as 'asn't changed much,"
he remarked slowly, while first Judy and then Bellman
emerged from under the settle, stretching themselves.

" Oh, an' wot's them ? " queried Mr. Bates,
looking up suspiciously.

" Why, the animals, Gawd bless 'em," returned
the old huntsman simply, and took his departure.
" Well, it's bin a grand outing," remarked Deacon—
his invariable comment—as they walked slowly up
the lane, and Judy and Bellman wagged eager assent.

After that they walked on in a companionable
silence. The old man and his two companions seemed
to melt into the dimness of the lane, the only points
of colour being the glow from Deacon's pipe and
Judy's white and Bellman's patchy coat, that could
just be seen as they trotted along, stopping every
now and then to sniff and sniff the elusive night smells
that conveyed to their questing noses secret and
delightful messages.

CHAPTER XVI

THE EARTH-STOPPERS

ONE night in the middle of September at about half-past ten, as Bellman lay comfortably dozing in the old arm-chair, he woke up with a start of surprise to see Deacon come in wearing his serviceable old mackintosh, an ancient felt hat, and round his neck a thick muffler. But what Bellman could not understand at all was the fact that under his arm the old man carried a short spade and a bill-hook. Close at his heels, and looking more important even than usual, was Judy. Evidently an outing of some sort. That was sufficient for Bellman, who immediately got on to his feet and stood waiting, ears and stern up, and a look in his mild eyes of keen expectancy. Deacon pretended great astonishment to see Bellman awake.

" 'Ello, wot are you gettin' yerself up outer bed for ? " he inquired, buttoning up his coat as he spoke.

" Because I'm coming with you, of course," replied Bellman's wagging stern, and with an air of saying, " why do you ask these silly, childish questions ? " But in order that there should be no possible mistake about the matter, he jumped down off the chair and took up a position near the door.

Deacon laughed outright and tucked the ends of his muffler in.

" Orl right, orl right," he said, " but you'll maybe wish as you was snug in yer bed agin, a tidy spell afore yer are."

Bellman took not the slightest notice of such a patently foolish remark, he merely stood woodenly waiting with an air of stolid patience until such time as Deacon should elect to start. At last all was ready ; before leaving, Deacon raked the fire together, and threw on some big lumps of coal, after which he unlatched the back door, and the three of them stepped out into the cool, damp September night. Bellman tilted his nose, and sniffed with keen appreciation.

It *was* a lovely night. The day had been one of those warm, mild ones of late summer, and now a light curtain of silver mist had drifted up and turned the trees and grass into a strange, pale, gossamer-like world. The dew lay thick and cold, and all about them was the first faint bitter-sweet tang of autumn. They crossed the stretch of heather where, in the pale grey light, the clumps of gorse looked like

They crossed the stretch of heather.

strangely-shaped sentinels of the moor standing silent and watchful. To-night Judy made no attempt to explore, but followed close on Deacon's heels, her tail at a sober downward angle, as though she knew that on this occasion she was on special duty.

Everything on the moor was still and quiet, the only sounds being the clink of the spade and bill-hook that Deacon carried, and the rattling swish of the short heather stems as Bellman and Judy plodded through. Just as they came to the little hunting-gate that led into the covert, there was the sound of the soft snapping of wet twigs, and Deacon stood still as a big dog-fox quitted the covert a few yards to the right of them. The old huntsman knew him well by sight; he had a torn ear and a jagged scar on his muzzle.

Whether or no the big fox had winded them, he made no sign, but stood a few seconds, his keen, sharply-pointed muzzle lifted, probing the secrets of the soft chill night air. Then, as though satisfied, with a flick of his white tagged brush he was away.

"Now, just wheer be yond chap bound for, I wonder?" murmured Deacon, releasing Bellman— he had laid a hand on the Beagle directly the big fox showed himself. "An' where 'as 'e left the wife an' kids, that's wot I want ter know?" he added.

Judy looked up impatiently—she was plainly anxious to start the night's work, and talking at the gate was getting them nowhere—she whined impatiently, and Deacon opened the gate, closing it silently after them again.

"I reckon," murmured the old man, shifting his bill-hook and spade to the other shoulder, "I reckon as we'd best mak' for t'main earth—up in t'dingle fust, eh, little bitch; wot's your notion?"

Judy was all for it; wagging her tail, she trotted briskly forward. The old earth up in the dingle was the property of the big dog-fox with the torn ear, whom they had just seen bound on some nefarious errand of his own, but what Deacon was anxious to know was the whereabouts of the vixen and five cubs. There was a steep rough way by which one could reach the dingle without walking up it. Deacon turned off the narrow path, and started to climb up the steep, slimy, clay bank. Fortunately there were ferns and bushes in plenty that made the climb a little easier than it otherwise would have been. But all the same it was warm work; however, the sight that met Deacon's eyes when at last he reached the top was well worth every inch of that long, toilsome scramble. Down in the bottom of the dingle five fine fox-cubs played light-heartedly, rolling each other

over, and darting in and out of the bracken and ferns
as they chased each other about the dingle.

A watery moon had risen and touched their tawny
jackets with delicate silver fingers. Deacon could see
the gleam of their sharp white teeth as they snarled
at each other in pretended anger. At a little distance
the vixen lay, paws outstretched, regarding the antics
of the youngsters with lazy satisfaction.

"Ay," muttered the old man under his breath,
"I don't wonder as ye're a bit set up with yerself
with that lot; you an' old lop-ear yonder 'ave done
the job proper, an' no mistake."

He crouched down, watching the cubs in silent
admiration, one hand on Bellman's neck in case that
worthy should suddenly take it into his head to make
closer investigations. Judy sat close beside Deacon,
her eyes fixed immovably on the gambolling cubs;
she was trembling in every limb, and the hair on her
back and neck rose stiffly, but she was a well-trained
little bitch, and she never once said a word. Just
below Deacon, on the slope of the dingle, sheltered
by an old tree root, was the earth.

As the old man made a slight movement, the spade
clinked against the bill-hook, and in that same moment
the dingle was empty; the bracken stems quivered
slightly, but that was all. Deacon blinked once or

In the bottom of the dingle five fox-cubs played light-heartedly.

twice. " Might as well get to work," he muttered, and scrambling down a little way into the dingle he picked up some fair-sized faggots of wood. These he arranged securely in the mouth of the earth, so that neither fox nor badger could shift them.

The work took some time, but Bellman didn't tire ; deeply interested, he watched the old huntsman's every movement. To " stop out " another smaller entrance to the earth was only the work of a few minutes, and then Deacon picked up his tools.

" There, I reckon that's all ship-shape against the 'ounds comin' in t'mornin'," he said, surveying his work with satisfaction. " But I reckon we'd better 'ave a look at that there old drain on top side," he added, descending to the path again and walking on.

Deacon made a very good earth-stopper, because, apart from his extensive knowledge of animals and their ways, he was painstaking and conscientious, sparing no efforts to do the job properly. This particular drain he was going to " stop out " permanently, as it was a source of constant annoyance to the fox - hunting contingent, and a well-used sanctuary for foxes in that part of the country.

As they walked quietly up one of the narrow " rides," a clumsy, ungainly shape crossed the path fifty yards in front of them.

"Yon's a rare sight," murmured Deacon, highly delighted and standing motionless until the badger had waddled away out of sight. "I've seen signs of 'em in plenty, but that be the first brock as I've clapped eye on i' this covert," he remarked, as they moved on again.

When they arrived at the old drain Judy's services were required, first of all, in order to see whether, before blocking up the entrance and exits, any unlucky rabbit or cub was hiding there. All eagerness, the little terrier bitch crept into the small hole that marked the mouth of the drain, and in a couple of seconds she had disappeared into the gloom. Bellman sniffed cautiously at the dark, narrow opening, but showed no desire to explore the black, damp tunnel beyond.

There was no sound from Judy, "nobody at 'ome seemin'ly," grunted Deacon, and a minute later Judy, emerging at the other end, confirmed his surmise. Her whiskers were earth-stained, and sticking to the hair on her legs and underneath her body were little clots of wet clay. She seemed rather disappointed with the result of her investigation, and lifted her lip shrewishly as Bellman peered interestedly down the hole from which she had just emerged. Deacon, meanwhile, had collected some heavy stones, and was scientifically blocking both entrances to the drain.

Before turning for home he " stopped " two more smaller earths. By the time they arrived back at the cottage, Bellman was quite glad to retire to the old arm-chair—Judy sat down close to the fire, she was feeling rather damp. Deacon put away his tools and hung up his hat and coat.

" 'Ungary work, earth-stoppin'," he remarked, putting the poker into the fire and walking off into the little pantry. Bellman immediately sat up interestedly ; earth-stopping *was* hungry work.

As Deacon returned, the Beagle quietly got down from the arm-chair and came up to the fireplace to get a closer view of the old man's movements. The latter carried a saucepan which he carefully placed on the fire. In a short time it started to bubble, and when Deacon lifted the lid, Bellman and Judy drew a little nearer—there was a wonderful scent coming from that saucepan.

Presently Deacon put out three plates and a loaf of bread, and, going into the pantry again, returned with a small jug of beer, Bellman watching his every movement with fascinated eyes. When the smell from the pot grew very strong and savoury, Deacon lifted the saucepan off the fire, withdrew the poker, now red hot, and plunged it hissing and sizzling into his jug of beer.

Then taking off the saucepan lid he started to ladle out the contents into the three plates, and Beagle and terrier drew nearer still. The mixture on the plates that was so tantalising the noses of Judy and Bellman was made from an old recipe of Deacon's own, and his one extravagance : bacon, kidneys, good lean beef, rice, and a couple of handfuls of mushrooms that Deacon had gathered that morning—pearly white, pink-lined " buttons," dewy cold and fresh—all boiled together in milk and butter. Just before it was ready, Deacon poured in a little port wine from a bottle the Master had given him.

All was now complete ; the old man took a long pull at the mulled ale, then placing two of the plates on the floor, he picked up the third, and, dipping a piece of bread in, he pulled his chair a little closer to the fire and began to eat. At that moment he would have changed places with no man, rich or poor ; and as for Judy and Bellman, what more could the simple hearts of dogs desire ? Limbs pleasantly tired, a warm hearth, savoury food, and the presence of their god.

The three earth-stoppers were very hungry ; in a short time the three plates were empty, and two of them were polished. There was still a little of the mulled ale left, and now Deacon drew out his old pipe and leaned back in his chair, at peace with all the world. Judy immediately jumped on to his knees, and curled up into a tight compact ball, short tail half-hiding her strong-scarred little muzzle, and in a very few minutes her dirt-encrusted eyes closed.

Bellman, after a covetous glance in Judy's direction, flopped down at Deacon's feet and dropped his head heavily across the old man's instep.

Deacon gazed into the fire and presently his grey head sank lower and lower until at last his chin rested on the old yellow " weskit," and he too dozed. Judy whined in her sleep, sharp querulous little whines that told of some hunt she was living over again. Bellman snuggled his frosty muzzle a bit closer over Deacon's foot and gave a little snore of contentment. At that moment the old huntsman opened his eyes and glanced down at the sleeping Beagle.

" We ain't so young as we once was, old lad," he murmured, " we maybe couldn't catch an 'are on our own now, but that don't mean as we're too old ter enjoy oursens a bit yet, I reckon, in our own way."

Bellman opened one eye and his stern thumped twice in emphatic agreement. Then with a little grunt of pure happiness he followed Judy into the land where dreams are made.